Murder in the Library

A mystery inspired by Sherlock Holmes and one of his most famous cases

Felicia Carparelli

First edition published in 2011

Paperback ISBN 9791908218407
Mobipocket/Kindle ISBN 9781908218414
ePub ISBN 9781908218421

Published in the UK by MX Publishing
335 Princess Park Manor, Royal Drive, London, N11 3GX
www.mxpublishing.com

Cover artwork by www.staunch.com

To Christine, Red, Tina, and Pete for all their support and and encouragement.

And to Christina Schultz, a very special thank you for her amazing editing and help with this manuscript.

It was a cool, autumn morning, one of those dawns when the air was chilled but the earth was still warm and the fog drifted in from Lake Michigan to infiltrate the north side of Chicago, with air as thick and white as cotton. It was 6 a.m., and I was walking my two dogs slowly up the street in front of my house. All was quiet except for the scrabbling of squirrels hidden in a tree. The fog was like a shroud and I shivered.

I looked over my shoulder. Was that a person lurking behind that maple tree? I would be an easy target with my hands full of dog leashes and plastic poop bags. If I were more like my Greek father I would call this a presage of events to come. The fog would be my personal oracle of Delphi, warning me of some cataclysmic personal doom. Instead, I have a lot of my Italian mother in me.

I cursed the fog, dared Jack the Ripper to come and get me and walked back to my house, dragging the sniffing pups up the stairs to my waiting coffee and their breakfast.

Chapter One

Beware of Greeks Bearing Gifts

-Virgil

My name is Violetta Aristotle. I am a librarian, not a philosopher. My father owns a restaurant in Chicago and my mother used to sing at the Lyric Opera. They named me after Violetta from Verdi's opera *La Traviata*.

I have always wanted to be a librarian. There is something so comforting about the smell of a new book; the pristine white pages practically glow and the aroma of the ink and paper is like fresh baked cookies to me. Even when I was a little girl I used to play library and would check out books to all my teddy bears. I don't know where I got this obsession, mom and dad are well-read, but not bookish, so I can't say it runs in the genes. But libraries are my passion, as were my late husband's. Some people like to say that libraries are a good place for eccentric people to work or to hide, and maybe they're right. You'll have to judge for yourself.

Chapter Two

Habeas Corpus

-Ancient Common Law

It was seven o'clock in the morning. The library was as silent as a tomb. Last night, the Midwestern University Library had hosted a party to celebrate a donation of rare Turkish and Sumerian art.

My department, the Reference and Reading Room, was not in as bad shape as I expected but we had a long way to go to make it habitable before the patrons arrived at nine o'clock.

My assistant, Scarlett, and I were sipping soy lattes and looking around the room. It was cold in here this morning and we had wisely kept our coats on. All the food and drink tables had been removed but the reading tables were still shoved aside, the chairs were everywhere and display cases and magazine racks all had to be put back into place. It was a big job for two people and we were waiting for two students from the university who worked as library pages and for the custodians to arrive.

"What time are they coming?" Scarlett asked me.

"I said we'd be here at 7 but I bet they don't show up until 8," I said. "But that's all right, we can figure out where we want everything to go. This might be a good time to rearrange the furniture."

Scarlett sighed. I was big on *feng shui* and trying to make the library more attractive. The library often received donations of carpets, chairs, lamps and *objets d'arts* and I always put a bid in for them so our department would be even more beautiful and stimulating to our readers. I loved plants and fresh flowers and the Reading Room always had blooms to reflect the season. This place was my second home and I loved it.

Last night we had been shocked when the current head of the library, Mrs. Lois Dalton Vandermeer, had announced she was going to Washington D.C. to work on a literacy committee and her replacement was going to be Hieronymus Wilde, the head of the History Department. Hieronymus was neither an artist nor clever as his name implied but a crashing bore, a womanizer and a very bad poet.

"I can't believe that Hieronymus is going to be the interim director," Scarlett said. "It's unbelievable. It should have been Peter, he has more seniority. And he is a much better administrator." Peter Lancaster was her boyfriend, also in the History Department. He hated Wilde for stealing an idea for heat sensitive book labels and selling it to Microsoft for big money. Peter was our resident Beethoven; wild haired and very dramatic in speech and behavior.

Personally I thought both Wilde and Peter Lancaster were both lousy administrators but prudently said nothing. Wilde promoted anybody who worshiped him and Peter was too disorganized to do a good job of either micro or macromanaging. I thought their assistants did most of the work.

"Yes, it is rather amazing, but Wilde has been playing up to Vandermeer for a couple of years, big time," I said. "Somehow he managed to fool her, too. I don't know how he does it, but he does. Some people find him charming. And intelligent."

"I did once," Scarlett said with a sigh. "How could I get drunk and sleep with him? I must have been mad."

"It was a temporary aberration brought on by the rich French and Cajun cuisine and the New Orleans aura," I said in her defense. The seduction had occurred during an American Library Association convention. "It could have happened to anybody."

"I wonder if he's going to immediately transfer Mark de Winter," Scarlett mused. Mark was the ex-husband of Wilde's mistress, Roxanne de Winter. No love lost, there.

"He might try, but Mark can file a grievance with the union," I said. "After all, Mark has a degree in Music, he's qualified."

"But Hieronymus is so devious, he could close his position, transfer him somewhere else, wait a while and then open the position again," Scarlett said. "I've seen it happen."

"Surely Wilde won't be interim director that long?" I said with a frown. "God, he'll make a mess of the library with his incompetence. The board of directors has got to advertise and hire a new director soon, won't they?"

"Let's hope so." Scarlett yawned. "Sorry, Violetta, but Peter was up all night fuming about Wilde."

"I can imagine," I said. "I couldn't sleep either, thinking about the changes about to take place here at the library."

Last night after the party I had eaten delicious lamb stew with my parents, walked my two *bichons* Samson and Delilah, and had sat up watching an old Norma Shearer-Robert Taylor movie until after midnight. Shearer had hired Taylor to masquerade as her boyfriend so she could make her real beau, George Sanders, become jealous and more attentive. She never planned on Taylor falling in love with her and complicating things. I would love those kind of complications but nothing exotic has happened to me in a long while.

Scarlett and I sat and sipped our lattes for a while and then I said, "Let's take a walk around and see if they picked up all the garbage."

We slowly made our way behind the enormous 30 foot mahogany circulation and reference desk built in 1910 and went to our small offices behind the stacks to put away our coats and bags. Outside my office was Hugo Haydn's desk. He was a new, young librarian who was very fond of me. He had a choice of several empty desks behind the reference counter but he had picked the one closest to me. On his very neat desk were a small crystal clock and an onyx pen holder. His three favorite books which he insisted were practically autobiographical lay in a neat stack. The books were *The Catcher in the Rye*, *The Hound of the Baskervilles* and *Auntie Mame*. I knew he had been raised by an outrageous elderly aunt who had once been in the circus, but I didn't think he resembled either Holden Caulfield or Sherlock Holmes.

Behind the desk ran dozens of vertical book stacks which held our reference collection, periodicals and newspapers and other materials like maps and phone books. Behind the desk there was very little to do, besides a couple of glasses and napkins that had been missed and three large trash bags that hadn't been picked up yet. All was quiet, all was serene. The morning light was beginning to glow through the stained glass windows and the floor was suffused with gem-like illuminations. I hadn't turned on the overhead lights yet and I was enjoying- no, basking in the glow of emerald and ruby light that danced over my very cool pink and black oxford pseudo- librarian shoes, with kitten heels, size 12.

"All's right with the world," I whispered and then stubbed my toe on a crushed bust of William Shakespeare which was lying on top of a particularly shocking piece of leftover trash.

At first I thought I had walked into a garbage bag that had fallen over on its side. Then I looked down and gasped.

"OH MY GOD!" I shrieked. "It's Hieronymus Wilde!"

Scarlett came running out of her office.

"What did you say?" she said. "Is something wrong?"

I motioned to the inert body of Wilde lying across a Chinese Deco rug donated by a society maven. He looked incongruous stretched across the purple carpet. His feet lay carelessly across an urn with flowers; a butterfly hovered around his left ear. A broken statue of Shakespeare lay in pieces around his body.

"Did he trip and knock himself out?" Scarlett asked, bending over him.

"He must have been drunk and crashed into the wall," I said. The niche in the wall where the statue normally resided was empty. I tapped his foot with my toe.

"Wilde... Hieronymus. Time to get up," I said. I nudged him again, this time with my whole foot. He felt very stiff and I knew something was terribly wrong.

I leaned over him. He wore an Armani suit which was covered in white plaster dust and he was lying next to his cherry wood walking stick topped with an ornate brass pineapple. Pretentious but effective. He was face down on the carpet and I couldn't tell if he was breathing. Carefully, I laid two fingers at the side of his neck. He felt stone cold. I pulled at his arm. No response.

"Hieronymus, oh dammit, Hieronymus, why did you have to die in my department?"

"You mean he's dead?" Scarlett gasped.

"I think so, sweetie," I said.

"Shouldn't we check first?"

"I suppose so," I grimaced and touched his arm again.

"Come on, Scarlett, give me a hand here," I said. "Let's roll him over."

"Oh God, Violetta, do we have to?"

"It's all right; he won't hurt us." Wilde's glorious head of thick, wavy auburn hair was matted on the top of his head and shining through was a particularly nasty looking lump, the size of a golf ball. "Looks like someone conked him on the head with the statue," I said with a grimace. "Maybe he's in a coma."

"Are you sure?"

I don't know, ***come on-"*** I almost yelled at her. "Let get this over with."

"All right," she said. "What should we do first?"

"I'll take the top of him and you take the bottom and we'll roll him over." I took his shoulder and arm and Scarlett grabbed a leg and thigh between her strong hands.

"One, two, three!" we groaned and rolled him over.

Hieronymus Wilde was indeed dead. He was stiff, wide-eyed and as cool as the room he had been lying in. His usual tan complexion was now as pale as the face of the bust of Milton.

I stared in horror. Scarlett covered her face with her hands.

"He looks so horrible," she said. "Like a monster."

"Indeed he does." His face looked frozen in pain and fear like he had just seen the Medusa and had turned to stone. I was very fond of Greek mythology but this situation was not fiction, it was real life and I was stuck in the middle of it.

I took a deep breath and whipped my cell phone out of my pocket.

I dialed 911.

"Please," I said, my voice wobbly, "please send the police and an ambulance to the Reference and Reading room of the Midwestern University Library. Someone has died."

Scarlett was peering at the body through her fingers. "Can't you close his eyes or something, Scarlett? He looks so terrible with his eyes open."

I have watched a million movies where the dead hero's eyes are closed tenderly by the attending doctor but I couldn't bring myself to do it. Instead I picked up a linen napkin from the circulation desk and placed it over his face.

"*Cover his face, mine eyes dazzle. He died young*," I misquoted the Duchess of Malfi and shivered.

"Stay right here," I told her. "I want to take a quick look around the department."

"You're going to leave me alone with him?" she asked. "And what if," her voice sunk to a stage whisper, "someone is still in here?"

"Listen, girlfriend, you've thrown out drunken undergraduates from this department, I'm sure you could subdue the corpse of Hieronymus Wilde, if you have to," I said with a bravado I wasn't quite feeling.

"Do you believe in the living dead?" she asked. "What if he starts to speak to me?"

"Tell him to keep quiet," I tossed over my shoulder. I ran across the hall. The History Department doors were open and the room was empty. I exhaled like I had a personal hurricane inside me and I realized my hands were shaking. What was I looking for? There was no one around.

I ran back across the hall. My square heels made little slapping noises on the marble floor. That was the only sound except for the wild beating of my heart. Scarlett hadn't moved a muscle. I quickly trotted around the perimeter of the room, looking down book stacks and under tables, just in case. I stuck my head under the circulation desk and heaven, help me, cast an eye into the book drop.

When I returned Scarlett was sitting on an oak library chair with Wilde's walking stick in her hands. She had a faraway look in her eyes.

"What are you doing?" I shrieked. "You're not supposed to touch anything!"

"Really?" She looked down at the stick and picked up a linen napkin from the floor. Wordlessly, she started rubbing the stick down with firm, smooth strokes.

"Now what are you doing?" I placed my hands upon my hips in amazement. What had happened to my usually clear headed friend?

"I'm erasing my fingerprints," she said.

"Yes, and his fingerprints, too," I hissed at her. "And maybe a murderer's."

"I never thought of that," she said, stuffing the napkin in the pocket of her sweater. "But why should my fingerprints have been on his stick?"

I looked at her for a second. She still had a strange look on her face. Why was she being so damned odd?

In the distance I heard the sound of an ambulance. My stomach started to lurch.

"Why shouldn't your fingerprints be on it? You could have picked it up last night at the party when it fell over, in fact, didn't I see you do that just a couple of days ago?"

She thought about it for a second and then shrugged. "Maybe so, but it's too late now. I wiped it clean."

I was about to look up how many years we would get for tampering with evidence but then another early arriving librarian walked into our department and let out a blood curdling scream.

Chapter Three

He is dead and gone Lady, he is dead and gone.

-Hamlet

I squeezed my eyes shut and listened to the cacophony of sound surrounding me. I heard the screams of the librarian from History, (definitely a contralto) as she ran back out of the room, the sounds of urgent voices coming from the elevator and the blare of sirens outside the building. It was an assault on my auditory nerves and I covered my ears with my still trembling hands. I was rudely poked in the stomach and my eyes flew open.

"Come on!" Now it was Scarlett's turn to take charge.

"What?"

"You can't stand here like a dummy!" Her fright had left her and she was brimming with energy and excitement.

"Why not?" I said. I made an executive decision. "OK, I'm going to the bathroom."

"Violetta," she said, grabbing my arm. "I'll go with you." I couldn't break out of her iron grip for love nor money. For the first time I realized that ex-serial cataloguers had extremely strong hands.

I really did have to use the bathroom and it seemed to take forever. Scarlett stood staring at her reflection in the gilt mirror hanging over the marble sink

"I can't believe he's dead!" she kept saying over and over.

She seemed unnaturally animated. I supposed it was shock. I mean, how many times does a man you have had an affair with get his head bashed in?

I washed my hands and put some cold water on a paper towel. I gingerly pressed the towel to the back of her neck.

She snapped to.

"Am I acting crazy?"

"It's OK, you're just in shock."

"I need a drink," she said.

"It's kind of early," I said dubiously, "but maybe someone has a flask around here." Librarians are notorious partiers.

I patted her shoulder and we started back down the hall.

When we returned our department looked like a set for CSI Miami. Paramedics and policemen were everywhere. There was a lot of noise and confusion. Elsie Walker, the contralto with the bloodcurdling screams, was laying prostrate on a stretcher breathing from an oxygen mask. Somewhere from the bowels of the building three real serials cataloguers had appeared; each one more hysterical than the last. Dolly Wilde, Wilde's widow, was thankfully not in sight. A few custodians were standing around, brooms in hand, talking softly. More people walked up to the entrance of the department, but by now, they were being asked to please move away from the doors.

We stood just inside the entrance half hidden behind a bust of Herodotus, the father of history. I discovered that Scarlett was still clutching me by the arm, just above the elbow and that my arm was starting to go numb from the pressure. I moved my hand.

"Scarlett," I whispered. "Scarlett! You're breaking my arm!"

"Sorry," Scarlett whispered back. "Why don't they take him away?"

The police were circling the body and it appeared that Hieronymus was not going anywhere. The paramedics packed up their belongings and made their exit. More police began to arrive and a photographer with bags of equipment. The lingering custodians and weeping serials cataloguing librarians were requested to leave.

I held my breath when the photographer leaned in and started taking pictures of Wilde's cherry wood walking stick. Even though I may be a meek and mild librarian I still appreciate the dangerous. I wondered who the detective was who was going to be leading this investigation and what he or she would think when they found no fingerprints on the walking stick. And I hoped to God, they wouldn't be able to tell we rolled him over. Somehow I think that was a police faux pas.

"Holy Mary Mother of God," I reverted to my Catholic school upbringing in times of extreme stress, "please save me and Scarlett from discovery."

"What are you mumbling about?" Scarlett hissed in my ear. "And will you take a look at that?"

That was a red-haired giant who had just strode into the Reference and Reading Room like he owned it. He was amazingly tall and he looked like he could smell a lie from 50 feet. He was rugged like a modern Abe Lincoln. He had an extremely sleepy and serious look on his face and I started to inch towards the exit, this time pulling Scarlett after me.

We had just skirted around old Herodotus and were walking out the door when a deep voice stopped us in our tracks.

"Excuse me ladies, would you wait up a minute?"

I turned and looked into the greenest eyes I have ever seen, outside of a cat. The rest of him was rather cat-like too, sinewy and slim, but he was more panther than house cat. The man looked dangerous.

"Yes, did you want something?" Scarlett asked. I could only stare.

God, is he gorgeous. How tall is he? 6 feet 7? 8? Is he married? How old is he?

His green eyes locked with mine for a fraction of a second.

Man, is she pretty, but that black dress and those shoes! Does she think she's a librarian?

"Ladies," the red-haired giant said in a deep, sensual voice, "I would like to talk to you for a minute."

I was sure guilt was plastered all over my frozen face. I opened my mouth but nothing happened. Good old Scarlett, boldly attired in a red dress with black boots, red lipstick perfectly in place, smiled up at him with true appreciation.

"How can we help you?" She was practically drawling like her namesake.

"Would you mind stepping over here for a minute," he said. "I have a couple of things I'd like to ask you."

Like what? I didn't like his imperious attitude.

"Like what?" I blurted out.

He smiled for a millisecond and his face didn't look quite so remote.

"Well, I know you work in this department and I'd like you to tell me exactly what happened when you came in this morning."

He motioned to us and we were escorted behind the reference desk. There a makeshift police office had been set up. People and equipment were everywhere. A couple of cases marked *Cook County Coroner's Office* were blocking our path. The giant neatly pushed them out of the way with a very large shoe and beckoned us to a corner of the work area.

He pulled a BlackBerry out of his pocket and poked at it with a long finger.

"Names, please?"

Scarlett and I exchanged a quick glance. The inquisition was about to begin.

"I'm Violetta-"

"Aristotle," he finished for me. "So you must be Scarlett Prendergast," he nodded at her.

"If you knew that already why did you ask?" I said, peeved at his presumption.

He gave me a look like I was an unruly child. "Just routine, ma'am."

"Just the facts, ma'am," I muttered under my breath.

He smiled again, briefly, but enough for us to see he could be human.

"Something like that," he said.

"How did you get our names?" Scarlett asked him.

"I got a list of people who have entered the library this morning from security," he explained. "You were the first two librarians to arrive this morning. Could you tell me why?"

"We wanted to clean up our department, there had been a party last night and everything had been rearranged," Scarlett said.

"And what is your position in the-" he looked at his BlackBerry again, "the Reference and Reading Room?"

"I'm the assistant head and Violetta is the head of the department."

He gave me a quick once over, glancing over my tall ample figure demurely clad in a vintage black cashmere sweater, black high necked but short sheath dress, black stockings and John Fluevog black and pink oxfords with big pink bows. My hair, which was very long and black and not been cut since my husband died five years ago, was arranged in a French twist, held with tortoise shell clips. He looked like he had my number and I didn't like it.

"You don't look like a librarian," he said. I've heard that before.

"No?" I said coldly. "What do I look like?"

"More like a headmistress of an exclusive school," he mused.

"Well, that's better than being called Morticia." I said wryly.

He coughed suspiciously. I decided to spare him.

"You don't look like a policeman," I said, casually. "You look like a gym teacher."

He smiled.

"My mother wanted me to become a teacher, but I opted for a career in law enforcement instead," he told us.

"Fascinating," I said in a low voice. Scarlett swallowed a giggle.

We waited while he consulted his notes.

"So, let's get back to this morning, ladies," he said. "Did you arrive together?"

"Yes-" I said.

"No-" Scarlett said. "Remember, Violetta? I went to the bathroom and you came in first."

"Right, you're right," I mumbled. He made notes, typing quickly without taking his eyes off of us.

"So you came in first, Ms. Aristotle?"

"Mrs.," I said. I usually don't make a big deal of it, but somehow with those unnerving green eyes upon me, I needed protection.

"Mrs.," he confirmed politely. "You came in and did what? Turned on the lights?"

"Yes- no, wait- the lights behind the desk were on but the rest of the room was dark."

"Is that typical?"

"No, usually all the lights are off. The custodians are supposed to leave the departments in darkness and leave the lights on in the halls and staircases," I said.

"Did you think that was odd?"

"No, I just thought-"

"Yes?"

"I just thought maybe the custodians had left the lights on after the party ended," I said.

"So you did what when you came in?"

"I went to my office to put my bags down, turned on my laptop, decided it was cold and didn't take off my coat. Then I came out to look around to see how much more we needed to clean and move furniture."

"And Ms. Prendergast- or is it Mrs.?"

"No, it's miss," she fairly drawled at him. I longed to kick her with my heavy duty size 12 foot but restrained myself.

"Miss Prendergast," he said pleasantly. "What did you do when you returned from the bathroom?"

"I went straight to my office and was getting set up when I heard her scream, isn't that right, Violetta?"

"Yes, that's right," I said. I shut my lips firmly. Enough with the Inquisition.

The giant graced us with a fleeting smile.

"Thank you ladies, you can go wait in the cafeteria. Someone will come to take your statements later."

"Statements?" Scarlett asked.

"Just the facts, ma'am," I said.

"Why us?" Scarlett asked.

"We're going to have to question everyone who was at the party last night and everyone who was in the library between 9 pm and this morning." He sighed. "It's going to take a lot of time."

Lois Dalton Vandermeer strode around the corner hands on hips. She was one of **the** Vandermeers, a family who owned half of Chicago. She had been appointed library director because of her vast connections. She had been raised in New Orleans and sounded every inch the refined, southern belle. "Could someone please tell me what's going on here?" She wore a Chanel suit with an immense carved gold flower on one shoulder. She did not sound like a chic, society maven this morning; she sounded pissed. Right behind her was her administrative assistant, a very short young man by the name of Cornell Hamilton. We called him Corny because he told bad jokes and always wore prissy bow ties and stammered when he was nervous.

"This is Mrs. Van- Vandermeer, director of the li-library, Corny said, looking very anxious.

"Yes, ma'am, I'm Mick McGuire, Detective, Chicago Police Department," he whipped out his badge and held it down in front of her eyes.

Mick McGuire? Who is he kidding? Nobody has a name like that. It sounds like a name for a leprechaun.

Lois Dalton Vandermeer looked up, saw she was speaking to an attractive man around 35, and dropped the bad attitude. Instead her hands fluttered up to her throat and she batted her eyelashes. She would have made a good Madame Butterfly; she had all the moves of a geisha.

"I am very distressed to hear about the accident that befell poor Mr. Wilde," she said. "What was it, a heart attack?"

"It's too early to say, ma'am," McGuire said blandly. "There will have to be an autopsy."

"Oh my," she said. Her eyes were steely. "And what is this I hear about the library not being able to open on time?"

"The library will have to remain closed until further notice," he said. "The crime lab has to cover the building first and everyone has to be interviewed."

"Crime lab?" she asked, raising her arched brows. "Who said anything about a crime?"

"Until we know the cause of death, we have to treat it as a suspicious circumstance," he explained. "And I will have to get a list of everyone at the party last night, ma'am."

She turned to Corny. "Get him one." She turned

back to McGuire. "I've already had the President of the university on the phone. He wants to know when the library will be back in business."

"I don't know, ma'am, but I would say it will have to stay closed for a couple of hours. Say 12 o'clock?"

"This is ridiculous." She looked up at the clock, it was 8:00. "Can't you be done here before nine?"

"We'll see, ma'am," he said, but his look was impassive and he was punching keys furiously.

"I will be talking to your supervisor- and the Mayor," she said and clicked away, her high heels beating a furious staccato on the marble floor.

"Come on, Scarlett," I said. "Let's get out of here."

He looked up at us. "This way, ladies," he said. "Could you please use the emergency exit behind the desk?"

So we're not even going to be able to see the "great man" one last time. I would have liked to have seen what they were doing to his body and to the walking stick. We started to leave and then another scream, this one, much higher in pitch, pierced the air.

"Oh, Hieronymus, Hieronymus," the hysterical voice of Dolly Wilde cried, "What has he done to you?"

Taking this as a reason *not* to leave, I turned back into the main room and found Dolly trying to throw herself on the corpse of her husband. Two uniformed policemen were trying to hold her back but she was slipping out of their grasp. She was wearing a red tartan cape and a red beret. Her grey blonde pageboy hairdo framed a kindly, but unglamorous face. Her cheeks were as crimson as her beret and her eyes wide with shock.

Scarlett and I rushed up to her. "Dolly, Dolly!" I cried. "It's all right, dear, we're here," I said soothingly. She stopped her struggles and threw her arms around me. "Oh, Violetta, he's finally killed him!"

Behind me, I heard Scarlett's gasp of horror.

"Who's killed him?" One of the detectives asked her.

But it was too late. Dolly slid to the ground, weeping, still clutching my arms. I sank down unceremoniously beside her, wrapping my arms around her plump body to comfort her.

I noticed Scarlett slipping away behind the reference desk, I noticed that Wilde's body had been put on a stretcher and was being covered up, and I noticed the amused look of Detective McGuire as he observed my long legs in black stockings sprawled on the floor. I tried to tug on my skirt and look as dignified as possible. This was no small feat as I sat crumpled on the floor holding a weeping woman while numerous city and county employees milled around us. Some of my hairclips had slipped and my hair was starting to cascade over my shoulders. I felt vulnerable and exposed and wished I had left with Scarlett when we had the chance.

I looked up just in time to see Mick McGuire looking at me with a quick, startled expression.

"Hieronymus, Hieronymus," Dolly kept calling out. I sat with her on the floor, patting her back like I was burping a baby. Finally a doctor from the University Hospital arrived with the ubiquitous black bag and spoke to Dolly by name.

She knew the doctor and responded quickly to his soft voice and gentle manner. After a few minutes she allowed herself to be raised up and escorted gently to a back room where she could weep in private.

I tried to rise up as gracefully as Giselle and went looking for one of my numerous hairclips that had fallen off during the emotional tussle. I couldn't find it anywhere and was starting to look under tables and the old card catalog, kept for strictly historic purposes under Vandermeer's orders, when the red-haired giant beckoned to me from behind the desk.

Who me? I mouthed silently.

Yes, yes, he nodded and held up a hair clip for my inspection.

I walked over to him with as much dignity as I could muster, being rumpled and wild-haired. I grabbed a rubber band from the counter and was starting to roll up my hair when he said, "no, leave it down, your hair looks glorious." I stopped, paralyzed by the softness in his voice.

Why did I say that? She's going to think I'm after her. Not very pro, McGuire.

Why was I stopping? His voice was hypnotic. I was turning into a zombrarian.

He was walking into a back workroom and I had to follow him to get my hair clip. I kept my hair down, but it made me feel vulnerable. Once inside, he closed the door and handed me my hairclip. I had already lost some of my composure and I was trying to hang on to what little remained of it. In the back of the room sat another man, in a wild plaid sports coat, striped shirt and polka dot tie quietly making notes.

"Snappy dresser," I said under my breath.

"Excuse me?" McGuire asked.

"I said I'm under a lot of pressure."

"Of course you are," he agreed and whipped out the darned BlackBerry.

"Mrs. Aristotle," he said. Without seeming to his eyes dropped to my ringless hands. I locked up my wedding rings along with my heart.

"It was Mrs. five years ago," I said. "I'm a widow."

"Sorry," he said. "You look so young."

"I'm 32," I said. *Now why did I say that? Why did the sight of his rugged face make me want to blurt out my guts to him? Careful, Vi, it's been a long time.*

A widow? She looks awfully young to be a widow. I'll have to check the records on this one.

"You look much younger. Would you mind waiting in here for a few minutes? I've got a couple of things I want to ask you."

He left me sitting in the workroom with the silent man. I pulled up a chair and positioned it by the door so I could see what was going on. I looked over my shoulder at my companion but he paid no attention to me. I waited expectantly. I was not disappointed. Presently a uniformed officer escorted Mark de Winter into one office and Roxanne de Winter into another. I could still hear Dolly weeping and talking down the hall. Scarlett did not return and I wondered if she was drinking bad coffee and eating a limp croissant in the university library cafeteria.

I heard some shouts and then Peter Lancaster came striding in, accompanied by two men. He looked as wild-haired as ever and his face was a mask of rage.

"This is preposterous!" he shouted. "How would I know that ass is dead? I demand my lawyer! I'm not going to sit here and be put through the wringer over a bunch of false accusations!"

McGuire raised his eyebrows a fraction and the two cops immediately spirited Lancaster away into another office.

I wondered what the police had learned in under an hour and who had talked. There was plenty to spill around here and I thought if anyone had a right to kill Wilde, it would be Lancaster. Wilde had stolen his idea, so he said, and had made money off of it. Wilde had never made Lancaster a partner. Men have killed for less.

I saw Mick McGuire walk by and heard him say, "This floor is sealed off. Get everybody who works in here ASAP. The rest of the library is open for business. The President called the Mayor and God help us if we deprive the students access to this university library." He saw me peeking around the corner and raised his eyebrows. I stuck out my tongue at him. He looked startled and then he quietly chuckled. *Good job, Violetta.*

I sat and sat and sat some more. I picked up yesterday's *Sun Times* and tried to do the Jumble and the crossword. Usually I'm pretty good at it but today I couldn't think straight. I watched the clock. Ten, fifteen, twenty minutes passed by. I was getting tired of cooling my heels and was about to ask the cop who I presumed was told to watch me if he wanted to play Poker or Hangman or something when McGuire strode in, shut the door and sat down in the chair next to me.

"You can go out now, McCarthy," he said to the man. "They need you downstairs." The man left without a word and I waited. McGuire was giving off vibes that seemed positively unfriendly.

I tried studying my fingernails for a while and then studied the clock on the wall. When that got old I turned and looked at him. He looked straight back at me without emotion and I knew something was up.

"So," I said.

"So," he said. "Are you going to tell me what really happened this morning?"

Chapter Four

Hear no evil, See no Evil, Speak no Evil

-Proverb, Three Wise Monkeys

I looked at him with a blank expression, at least blank for me. This means I wasn't laughing or wringing my hands and getting mad and sputtering Greek and Italian curses. Instead, I got up and went over to the work station. I picked up a rubber band and slowly twisted my hair into a lopsided chignon. Then I picked up two chopsticks out of someone's leftover lunch bag and stuck them into my hair, securing the chignon to my head. I probably looked like *Turandot* after a wild bender in Shanghai.

"What are you talking about? I told you everything I know. I came in here this morning, stumbled upon Mr. Wilde, screamed, Scarlett came running and we called 911."

"Did you touch the body?"

I was still arranging my hair and he motioned politely for me to sit down. I sank down as gracefully as I could into the chair. I ignored his question and instead focused my eyes on the chipped plaster behind his head. I gasped when two strong hands grabbed the sides of the chair and turned me around to face him. The look on his face was not encouraging.

"Now look," he said softly, "we can play this game where you act like you don't know and I try to trap you into little indiscretions or we can open up and be upfront with each other like two mature adults."

Is that a cleft in his chin? How Kirk Douglas can you get? I wonder what he'd be like to make love to... He's not wearing a wedding ring.

Why does she look so innocent and sexy? I want to take her to bed for three days. Quit it, McGuire, it's been too damn long.

"Indiscretions," I repeated, idiotically. I was trying to think of something good to say, but it wasn't happening.

"Yes, indiscretions," he said. "Now look, Miss-Mrs. Aristotle, I know you are an intelligent, albeit sorrowful librarian, so let's not beat around the bush."

A cop who says albeit? What, is he Einstein?

"What bush?" I asked "George Bush? You're in the right place. This being a university and a library and all." My voice died away as I looked at his face.

He looked furious. His face had a mulish look and I knew I couldn't keep up this inane repartee forever. *Say something, stupid.*

Hugo Haydn came bounding through the door.

"Oh, Violetta, I mean Miss, Ms. Aristotle- are you OK? The police aren't bothering or harassing you, are they?" He sent a ferocious look at McGuire. My knight in shining armor was dressed in a Kelly green cashmere sweater, a pink shirt and black and white polka dot tie. He was wearing jeans and magenta and black striped Nikes.

"Snappy dresser," McGuire said under his breath. I choked back a laugh. The mood lightened immediately.

I ignored McGuire. "I'm fine, Hugo, just great. I'm just talking to the detective here; he's asking me some questions."

Hugo studied my face for a minute and then sighed. "If you say so. I'm just next door if you need me.

Would you like some coffee?" He wore wire-rimmed glasses and his strawberry blonde hair was brushed up into little feathery spikes. Hugo always reminded me of a punk Pee-Wee Herman.

"Bless you, Hugo, I believe I would."

McGuire jumped up. "I'll get it, please go back to your room, sir."

Hugo looked way up at McGuire and raised his eyebrows at me. He left the room and I relaxed. The things Hugo could tell them about our little band of librarians would probably get us all in jail before the day was over.

McGuire came back with a tray. He pulled up a chair and set it down. There were two cups of coffee and some doughnuts and a plate of saltines. I raised my eyebrows in amazement.

"Such service, I didn't expect the red carpet treatment from Chicago's finest."

"You probably are weak from shock," he said. I looked at him closely to see if he was being sarcastic but I couldn't read him that well. He was too new and too unknown for my emotional radar to pick up nuances.

He put a cup of coffee on the desk. "Cream? Sugar?"

"I'll take a Splenda," I said. He handed me one and then picked up the plate of doughnuts.

"Doughnut?"

I never eat doughnuts because they give me indigestion but this morning I could have eaten a half dozen without regret.

"Yes, please," I said without hesitation.

He waited. "Which one?"

"You pick," I said. He put a chocolate glazed doughnut on a napkin and put it in front of me. My, weren't we getting cozy. I eyed the hot coffee and doughnut and sighed.

"Can I go to the bathroom?" I asked.

"If you wish," he said, "I'll get a female officer to take you."

"Why?"

He shrugged. "Police procedure."

"You think I'm going to stuff valuable evidence down the toilet," I said. "Oh, never mind."

I picked up the coffee and drank gratefully and ate two bites of doughnut. "Heaven help me later, but I'm going to enjoy this."

"Not part of your regular diet, caffeine and sugar?" he smiled.

"Not really, I'm more of a tea and whole grain sort of girl," I said.

"Me, too," he said. "But if you're a cop you live on coffee, doughnuts and fast food."

"You look healthy," I said.

"On my days off I run and lift weights and I'm trying to eat more complex carbohydrates and low-fat protein, like brown rice and salmon," he explained. "I'm trying to build up my muscle mass."

He looked pretty muscular to me. "I see," I said. "So you're a clean living kind of guy."

"Something like that."

"Ever drink?"

"Once in a while."

"Smoke?"

"Never."

"What, no vices?" I asked.

"I like talking to librarians with long hair," he said.

I felt the room rock for a second. Must be the damned caffeine. I put the coffee cup down with a thump.

"This is all very fascinating conversation," I said, "but aren't you supposed to be interviewing me?"

He leaned back in his chair and looked at the BlackBerry.

"I thought I would soften you up, before you opened up," he said. "Remember? You were going to be honest with me?"

"I was?" I sure didn't remember a thing. "I think you were saying something about me not telling you everything I know."

"Yes, that was my original question," he said. "Was Mr. Wilde on his back when you found him?"

I paused then decided to be truthful. "He was on his stomach."

"And you turned him over?"

"Yes, Scarlett helped me."

"She did?"

"Well, I know I'm a big woman but he was not a lightweight."

"You're not that big," he said softly.

The room shifted again. Damn.

"So you turned him over and then what?"

"We turned him over to see if he was alive or in a coma or-"

"Dead?"

I shifted uncomfortably in my seat. "Yes. How do you know Wilde was moved?"

"Little things told us," he said softly. He was watching my face, which I'm sure by now was flushed with the coffee and with anxiety.

“Like what?” I asked

“First of all, when we were checking the body we saw his clothes were rumpled up in the back. And there were finger marks on his legs and shoulders like he had been recently grabbed.”

“Amazing,” I said. *But what about the cane?*

“There was also a scuff mark on his shoe that matched a spot on the floor,” he continued blandly. “There’s a lot of information that can be gleamed by the trained eye.”

The pompous ass. “Elementary, my dear Watson,” I said.

“Indubitably,” he agreed. “Now perhaps you can tell me about the cane.”

“The cane?” Now this was getting tricky.

“Yes, did you move his walking stick, a cherry wood cane with a brass pineapple on top.”

“No, it was laying next to his body.”

“You didn’t touch it?”

“No, I did not.”

“How about Ms. Prendergast?”

“I didn’t see her touch it,” I lied.

“Are you sure?”

“Maybe she touched it when we rolled the body over, I can’t be sure.”

He nodded. I wondered what Scarlett has told him.

“You will check the cane for prints, I imagine?” I tried to sound cool.

“You imagine correctly,” he said. He looked at me again, emerald eyes with just a speck of yellow. Cat’s eyes.

"The cane appeared to be wiped clean, but we're confident we will retrieve some prints when we get it to the lab."

"This is better than television," I said. "Anything else?"

"There were some of Wilde's hairs and a bit of blood found on the purple carpet in your library. Probably from when you rolled him over. Antique?"

"Wilde?"

"The rug," he said gently. *Stupido.*

"Chinese deco," I said, "from around 1930."

"Very nice," he said. "I like your department; it's very classy."

"Thank you," I said demurely, eyes down on the pink laces on my shoes.

"Miss Aristotle, level with me," he said. "Is there anything you're not telling me?"

I hesitated and then plunged in.

"OK, I'll tell you. I came in early this morning and was sitting there thinking about life. It's so nice and quiet in the library, first thing in the morning, it's like church. I was looking to see if any trash had been missed from last night's party and I stubbed my toe on Wilde. And I said to myself, why did he have to go get murdered in my department!"

"Oh, you knew it was murder, did you?" McGuire asked.

"No, not really, I at first thought he was drunk, hit his head and passed out."

"And then what made you change your mind?

"When I tapped his leg with my foot, it felt as stiff as a board. Rigor mortis, I guess."

"I guess so," he agreed.

"And he had a lump on his head that looked nasty."

"So then-"

"So then I got Scarlett to help me turn him over."

"Were you fond of Mr. Wilde?" he was typing in his BlackBerry the whole time I was speaking and I wondered if he was taking it all down verbatim, like they do on Perry Mason.

"No, not especially," I said.

"Why not?"

"Just didn't like him," I said. "He was pompous and arrogant and he thought all women loved him."

"And you didn't?"

"Certainly not!" I protested.

"But others did?"

"He could be charming at times," I conceded. "He quoted poetry at them."

"Don't like poetry?" he asked pleasantly.

"Poems are fine, it's the poets that can get on my nerves," I said, tugging my skirt down again.

He swallowed a smile and I felt my cheeks grow warm.

"Poets seem to do all right. Wilde had a wife and a mistress," McGuire said blandly.

I looked at the clock. It was only nine o'clock. In an hour he had found out some valuable dirt.

"Yes, I believe so," I agreed.

"And they both work in the library."

"Yes, we're just one big happy family here," I said. "One for all and all for one."

"Speaking of Musketeers," he said, "what is the name of the librarian with the scar on his face, the one who dueled with Wilde?"

"Mark de Winter," I blurted out. "Are you a psychic?" I demanded. "Where are you getting all this stuff?"

"Security and the custodial staff have been very helpful in setting up the dramatis personae of the department," he said.

"I've never heard a policeman with such a big vocabulary," I said.

"I've never met a librarian with so short a skirt," he said.

"Does it bug you?" I said, but tugged it down a fraction of an inch.

He glanced at my legs for a moment and then met my eyes. His emerald eyes locked with my big black pools of Mediterranean mush. I felt my heart beat quicker. I couldn't think straight. He was too close for comfort. Was this professional? Why was I spilling my guts out to a policeman when I had vowed to take the secret of moving Wilde's body to the grave?

"No, it doesn't," he said.

"Doesn't what?"

"Bug me," he said and damn it, he winked at me.

Chapter Five

Ask me no questions, I'll tell you no lies.

-Oliver Goldsmith

Mick McGuire sat at a mahogany desk talking to his right hand man, Sgt. O'Leary. They had suffered two years of Irish jokes since they started working together. McGuire and O'Leary were grand old names that evoked the Emerald Isle, Guinness Stout and the Chicago Fire, thanks to Mrs. O'Leary's cow kicking over a kerosene lantern in a barn way back in 1871. As a team they worked very well. O'Leary was about 10 years older than McGuire. They had a brotherly rapport that made them seem pleasant and a wee bit slow on the uptake. This south side charm (both were White Sox fans) had disarmed several murderers into blurting out valuable information.

Dolly Wilde was led in first. She was holding a snow white, crumpled handkerchief in her plump fingers and her face was as crumpled as the cloth, from emotion and crying. The policewoman pulled out a chair and gently pushed Dolly into the upholstered seat. McGuire eyed her pleasantly; O'Leary took out his notebook and kept chewing at the ever present toothpick he used as a substitute for cigarettes. "Mrs. Wilde?" Mick said quietly. She nodded and blew her nose.

"I'm Detective McGuire and this is Sergeant O'Leary. We'd like to ask you a few questions. I know this has been a terrible day for you and we don't want to keep you any longer than necessary."

Dolly nodded again and briefly closed her eyes. That one simple movement made McGuire uncomfortable.

He hated interviewing grieving widows, if she truly was one. Grief should not have to be discussed in a stuffy room under fluorescent lights.

"Mrs. Wilde," Mick cleared his throat and spoke softly. "We're very sorry for your loss."

"Thank you," she said. "What can I possibly tell you about-" She looked ready to cry again.

"If you could just remember when you last saw your husband it would help our investigation."

"What time did he come home?" O'Leary asked quietly, rearranging his toothpick.

Mick shot O'Leary a quick look and shook his head. *Not so fast.*

Dolly looked confused for a moment and then started tugging at the lace on her handkerchief.

"I'm not really sure," she whispered. "I take a sleeping pill at night and sleep very heavily."

The two men exchanged a glance. "What time did you get to bed last night?" Mick asked carefully.

"I was so keyed up after the wonderful party, that when I got home I took a hot shower, warmed up some milk, took my pill and tried to read a bit before I could fall asleep. I must have fallen asleep sometime after 11."

"Did you drive home with your husband?" Mick asked.

"No, I took a taxi home. We came in a taxi, too. We don't like to drive after we've been drinking. Dear Hieronymus is- was- is so fond of parties. He often came home much later than I."

"When you woke up this morning-"

"He had already left for the library. I know how honored he was to become the new director. He was so anxious to assume his duties."

"So the last time you spoke to him was last night?"

"Yes, that's right. Sometime at the end of the party. After Mrs. Vandermeer's speech. That was the last time." Her eyes welled up again and she daubed at her eyelids.

"Thank you, Mrs. Wilde," Mick said. "I'm sure you would like to go home now."

The policewoman helped her out of the chair. Both Mick and O'Leary rose to their feet.

"Where is he?" she asked tremulously. "Can I see him?"

"He's in good hands," Mick said. "Right now, he needs to be examined and then tomorrow morning, we'll call you so you can make the necessary arrangements." He hoped he sounded caring. The words sounded so cold.

She nodded. "Thank you," she whispered. She walked out with dignity.

Mick let out a sigh. Widows were the worst.

"Are you buying that?" O'Leary asked taking out his toothpick to inspect it.

"That Wilde left early this morning?"

"How about did Wilde come home at all last night?"

The two men looked at each other speculatively and then Roxanne de Winter was brought in for questioning.

She was pale but composed. She was wearing a grey suit and pearls. Her eyes were pink and she held a small packet of tissues in her hands.

"Please sit down," Mick said and introduced himself and the sergeant.

Roxanne nodded politely and touched the tissue to her eyes. She was very blonde and slim. All her gestures and movements were graceful, like a ballet dancer. She had a long swan-like neck and she always wore pearls. Some of the junior librarians called her Grace Kelly behind her back.

"I know this is a terrible shock-"

"Poor Hieronymus," she said, tears welling up in her eyes. "What a terrible accident!" The two men exchanged a brief look. "I'm always saying that some of the statues in this library are placed in too high and precarious spots. Why only yesterday, the bust of Chaucer was nearly knocked off its pedestal by a group of boy scouts and now this-" She sniffled delicately into the tissue.

"What time did you last see Mr. Wilde last night?" Mick asked pleasantly.

She sat up a little straighter and wrinkled her perfect little nose.

"See him? You mean at the party?"

"Yes, or after, if that's the case," McGuire said.

"Why would I see him after?" she said faintly, raising penciled brows.

"I don't know, ma'am, you tell us," Mick said, never taking his eyes off her pale face.

"I saw him at the end of the party, talking to Mrs. Vandermeer. I said good night to them both and then went home."

"By taxi?"

"No, I had my car," she said.

"Did you go home alone?"

She raised her brows again.

"I mean, did you give anyone else a ride home?"

She shook her head. "No, I didn't. I went right home and to bed. I had a splitting headache."

"What was your relationship with Mr. Wilde like?" She froze for an instant and then resumed patting her eyes.

"What do you mean? My working relationship?"

Mick nodded.

"We always were pleasant when we saw each other. We worked in different departments so our paths didn't cross many times during the day," she mused. "And of course, his wife Dolly and I are great friends. She is such a dear."

Mick wondered why she sounded like a character in a play. Her facial expressions were so guarded and her voice carefully modulated. Even the way she cried seemed staged.

She was either telling the truth or she was an excellent liar. His next interview seemed to corroborate the latter.

Mark de Winter was wide-eyed, angry and crumpled. He wore an oddly fitting pin-striped suit that looked too small for him. He had a short, compact body like a weight lifter. He walked forcefully into the room like a man who had just fought a duel and won. After throwing himself into the chair his ex-wife had vacated he challenged the two men.

"So do you want to know who really killed the old bastard?"

Both Mick and O'Leary started at the vehemence in his words.

"Sure, if you want to tell us," Mick said affably.

"Probably everybody! We all hated his phony guts."

"You more than others?" McGuire asked.

"Maybe." Now he was getting cagey.

"Would you like to tell us why people hated Wilde?"

"The usual reasons. Adultery, theft, fraud, gluttony, greed, lust- and just being a general ass." De Winter seemed happier now that he was trashing the dead man.

"A seven deadly sins sort of guy?" Mick asked.

"Precisely," de Winter smirked.

"Are these just idle rumors?"

"Wilde has been sleeping with my ex for years, that's not an idle rumor," de Winter said.

"With Roxanne de Winter?"

"All the time."

"Could Wilde have been with Mrs. de Winter last night?"

"Probably. He often spent the night with her."

"*Oh the tangled web we weave when we set out to deceive*," Mick intoned. "What did Mrs. Wilde think about that?"

Mark looked surprised. "Not many people quote Sir Walter Scott anymore. Ever been a librarian?" He grinned and McGuire could see a somewhat decent looking and acting man lurking behind the hurt and jealousy.

"In another life, perhaps," Mick smiled back. *Keep talking.*

"And Mrs. Wilde?" he prompted.

"She knew all right but she never said or did anything about it. As long as Wilde was hers most of the time, she put up with it."

"I just interviewed Mrs. Wilde and Mrs. de Winter," Mick said.

"They won't tell you a thing," he scoffed. "Their precious dignity must be preserved at all cost."

"How do we know that you're telling the truth?" O'Leary took the toothpick out of his mouth to ask.

Mark de Winter stared at O'Leary like he had just noticed him for the first time.

"You don't," he laughed.

"Where did you get the scar?"

"I ran into a wall?" he laughed again, with more enjoyment. McGuire wondered if he was still drunk from last night. Or maybe high? His pupils were dilated and he was jumpy. Librarians on coke? Was nothing sacred?

"Maybe you ran into a sword," Mick said.

"Maybe."

"And maybe that made you angry."

"Keep going, it's a good plot," de Winter said appreciatively.

"Maybe you were so jealous about Wilde sleeping with your ex-wife when you still wanted her that you bashed him over the head with a statue of Shakespeare last night after the party," Mick said.

"It makes a good story," de Winter said with another smirk. He passed a tired hand across his face. His hand shook slightly.

"Are you totally wasted?" Mick asked.

"Do I need a lawyer?"

"Not yet," Mick said. "Don't leave town."

"Gee, just like in the movies," de Winter said with another smirk.

Get outta here before I smash you in the face. Aw, hell. Whenever I start thinking like Tony Soprano it's time to move on.

"We'll be in touch," Mick dismissed him.

Peter Lancaster was smoldering. He was in control but you could see that he was furious.

"How could he die before our litigation was settled?" he asked the detectives the minute he came into the room. "If this ties things up even longer, I'm going to,"

"Kill him?" asked O'Leary blandly.

"That's what you think, isn't it? That I hit him over the head because he owed me money!"

"We-"

"To hell with what you think!"

McGuire opened his mouth to reply, but Lancaster was gone. He raised his eyebrows at O'Leary and got a thumbs down sign in return. This was going to be a hell of a day.

Hugo Haydn came in with a bound and a skip. He looked expectantly at both men. His spiky hair seemed to quiver with excitement. Mick swallowed a groan and tried not to look at O'Leary.

"Hugo Haydn?" he asked pleasantly.

"Yes, that's right, that's I, I mean that's me," he said smiling and rolling his eyes.

Was he for real?

"When was the last time you saw Hieronymus Wilde alive last night?"

Hugo squealed a bit in delight. "Ooooh, what a way to put it! I mean, how can I remember? I saw dear old Hieronymus, I mean Mr. Wilde, all over the place last night! Talking to this one, schmoozing with that one, and all the time, eating, drinking and being followed around by the ladies." He pronounced it lay-deez and Mick thought he might be from the south, with his hint of a drawl.

“Which ladies?” Mick asked. He watched Hugo without actually looking at him, and found him just as annoying.

“Oh my, have you got time?” Hugo rolled his eyes again and snickered. “Why, practically everybody who worked at the library. They all fell under the spell of *le grande* Wilde.” His French accent was curious, part Brooklyn, part Mississippi delta.

“Why was that?”

“Didn’t you see him? No, of course you didn’t, you only saw him dead,” Hugo said with wide eyes. “He was the romantic type of course, long locks, cashmere capes, always spouting poetry- women dig it.”

Do you? Mick wanted to ask, but left that out.

“How about Roxanne de Winter?”

“Oh, she’s devastated, simply ruined, now that Wilde’s gone. She might even have to go back to her ex,” he sniggered and Wilde thought he was one of the most unpleasant young pups he had seen in a long while.

“Were they getting along?”

“How do you mean?” Hugo looked innocent.

“I mean, if Roxanne was seeing Wilde and maybe wanted him to leave his wife for her, there could have been bad blood.”

“Enough for her to smack him over the head with the bust of Will Shakespeare, is that what you mean?” Hugo looked thrilled.

“Something like that,” Mick said blandly.

“Well, I suppose that could be, but I don’t really think so. Wilde would never have divorced Dolly; I mean how often can a man find such an eager, willing slave in his lifetime? No, I think he just would have fooled around with Roxanne, indefinitely, at least until someone younger came along."

"How old are you?" O'Leary asked.

"22."

"You're awfully jaded for someone so young," Mick said. "Don't think much about women?"

"I love women, some of my best friends are women," he said peevishly. "I don't know what you're driving at."

Mick dropped it.

"Are you friends with Mrs. Aristotle?"

Hugo beamed. "She's my very best friend."

Oh, is she?

"We're always going out for drinks and dinner," Hugo boasted.

"How nice," Mick said. "She's a widow, isn't she?"

"Why yes, her husband died of cancer five years ago, isn't that terrible? And she hasn't cut her hair or dated since then. Except for me," he said proudly. "And she always wears black. I'm trying to get her to start wearing some colors."

Check hospital records and death certificate. Mick made a note. Just routine, right? He didn't really think she *wasn't* a widow, now did he?

"She's lucky to have such a devoted friend," he said blandly. "How about Ms. Prendergast?"

"Scarlett?" Hugo laughed. "Our scarlet clad Scarlett with the scarlet hair?" He laughed again, amused at his feeble attempt at wit.

"Did she get along with Wilde?"

"Get along? Well, if one is to believe all the rumors," he leaned in, "they once had a fling in New

Orleans and Scarlett got her feelings hurt. And that's another reason Lancaster hates him so much, except Scarlett isn't supposed to know that he knows."

"And how do you know?" O'Leary asked.

"People just love to tell me things," Hugo said with a satisfied smile.

"I see you worked in Wilde's department for a week and then were transferred to the Reference and Reading Room."

Hugo coughed and turned pink. He swallowed and ran his hands through his spiky hair. "My, my, what long ears you have, Detective."

"The better to hear things with," Mick said pleasantly. "Why did you transfer? Didn't get along with Wilde?"

"Certainly not!" Hugo snapped. "There were more vacancies in Reference than History so the director moved some of us around, that's all."

"Thank you, Mr. Haydn, please go wait with the others outside," Mick said and stood up. He towered over Hugo by a foot. Hugo seemed fascinated by the difference in their heights but for once was silent. He flitted out of the room and Mick let out a sigh.

"One more," O'Leary said. "The other grave robber." He looked amused.

Scarlett Prendergast was very cordial. She entered the room with a click-click of her high-heeled boots and sat down with a rueful smile.

"How can I help you?" she purred in her best reference librarian voice.

O'Leary sat up and took the toothpick out of his mouth. Mick smiled.

"This is a terrible day for the library," he said.

"Horrible, nothing like this has ever happened here," she said, shaking her head sadly.

"Did you like Wilde?" Mick asked, throwing her one of his famous curves.

She froze and arranged her face again in a smile.

"Well, of course, we were colleagues. Why do you ask?"

"We know there was some trouble between Wilde and your friend Peter Lancaster," Mick said.

She seemed to relax a bit. "Yes, there was. Is. The litigation is still pending."

"Of course now with Wilde gone, things might change some," Mick said.

"Perhaps, maybe Dolly will settle the lawsuit," she said. "I hope so."

"Is that possible?" Mick asked.

"Dolly is not as mercenary as Wilde," Scarlett said. "I'm sure she will understand how Peter and Hieronymus worked together in creating their invention."

"I hear Wilde was quite a ladies' man," Mick said quietly.

She stiffened but attempted a smile. "Oh, he was all charm and poetry."

"Roxanne de Winter was his mistress."

"Mistress," Scarlett mused. "What an old-fashioned word."

"You prefer girlfriend? Amour? Lady friend?"

"I don't have a preference," she said.

"What did you think when you touched Wilde's body in the reference room this morning? Were you shocked?"

"Oh, yes," she said. "I just couldn't believe it-" She stopped, horrified and looked confused. "I mean, don't you mean when we found him in here?" She coughed and didn't look Mick or O'Leary in the eye.

"Thank you for your time," Mick said. "We'll be in touch."

She stood up and smoothed out her dress. Her look of shock and consternation was almost as funny as the admiring gaze in O'Leary's baby blue eyes.

Chapter Six

There'll be a hot time in the old town tonight.

-Song, 1886.

I watched librarians coming and going out of McGuire's interview room for a long time. Everyone looked subdued except for Hugo. He seemed to be enjoying the attention and I'm sure along with Dolly Wilde he had blabbed out every piece of gossip he had ever heard since he started working here.

I was allowed to go to the bathroom with a uniformed female police officer who was quite nice and told me she liked my shoes. She had two kids, ages 11 and 15, and she was trying to work her way up to being a detective like McGuire. She told me he had a fine mind for investigative work. His body wasn't so bad either.

I was turning into a lusty, sex-starved librarian. Just because I had been forced to sit in a small room with such a big man reeking of testosterone and lime aftershave I was losing my control. Siegfried had been my angel, my *cheri amour*, but he had been gone for five years and I had forgotten what it was like to be held by a man.

It was almost noon when we were asked to go into the main room of the History Department. Everyone was assembled there, all the librarians from History, Literature, the Reference and Reading Room and Fine Arts, the four departments on this floor. Dolly Wilde was not present and I assumed she had been taken home to cope with her grief. Wilde's remains had been removed and most of the police equipment was gone. The back of the room was filled with policemen and detectives. The doors were shut. We sat and waited. Scarlett was sitting across the room from me and I leaned over in my seat, made eye contact with her and raised my eyebrows. She did likewise and I gave a nervous laugh.

McGuire walked through the group of librarians. He stood in front of the circulation desk, towering over everybody in the room. He started to speak and I noticed his deep sexy voice carried quite well without a microphone. His diction was very good and I wondered where he had grown up and gone to college.

"Ladies and Gentleman," he began, "thank you for your patience today. I know this has been a particularly stressful and sad day for you all. At the moment we are treating Mr. Wilde's death as a possible homicide." An enormous collective gasp went around the library. Roxanne de Winter started to sniffle into a white, lace handkerchief.

"Why do you say that?" One of the young history groupies asked McGuire. "Didn't he fall down and hit his head?"

"Or did he hit his head and fall down?" I whispered to Hugo. He squeezed my hand reassuringly. He looked very pale and very excited.

"It's too early to say," McGuire said. "We have to wait until the body has been examined more closely. There might be a possibility of foul play. We'll know more later today."

"How long are you going to keep us locked up in here?" Peter Lancaster demanded. He looked very angry and more like Beethoven than ever. "Are we all under arrest?"

"No one is under arrest," McGuire said without emotion. "You are all free to go back to your departments and finish the rest of the day."

"Why can't we leave?" Lancaster demanded again. "You *are* holding us."

"We are not holding anyone," McGuire said. "We're sorry if you felt you were being accused. We were just trying to get some vital information about the staff and their relations with Mr. Wilde."

"You just wanted to know who was sleeping with whom," Mark de Winter shot out. "You wanted to know who didn't like Wilde and the answer is everybody!"

I held my breath. McGuire ignored that remark.

"You can go now," he repeated. "Thanks again for your cooperation."

"We can go home?" a young Music Department librarian asked.

Mc Guire smiled. "It's OK with me but since you are library employees if you want to leave early you will have to ask your supervisor for permission."

I wondered what Mrs. Vandermeer would say if we all stormed upstairs to her ornate office with the Persian rugs and Chippendale desk and demanded to go home.

The great man had spoken. We could go. Some of us got up immediately, others remained seated. There was an air of unreality in the room and there was quiet, speculative talk among us. Roxanne was still weeping and her ex-husband Mark had his arm around her and was talking quietly. Scarlett had her arm on Peter's arm as if to subdue any further outbursts.

Our floor was going to remain closed the rest of the day, I heard a detective say as we all dispersed into our own departments. I was tired, I was depressed, I was afraid I would have to go downtown and get my father to come bail me out. McGuire had made a point of telling me he would look for me later. I walked across the hall and looked for Scarlett.

She was still talking to Lancaster, but after a minute, he shook his head angrily and stormed out of our department. When she saw me, she pulled me into her office and closed the door.

"Peter is so mad," she said, "the police implied that he had an argument with Wilde and hit him over the head. Everyone knows about how Wilde stole his invention. And some of them won't stop talking about it." Now it was her turn to look furious.

"I know" I agreed. "They seem to know an awful lot about us in a very short amount of time."

"Please don't be mad at me, Violetta, but I think I spilled the beans about us finding Wilde's body. That policeman, with his lazy green eyes, just bewitched me and I blurted out the truth," she said looking stricken.

I sat down and pulled the sticks and rubber bands out of my hair. I put my face in my hands and groaned.

"What's the matter?"

"I'm afraid I'm the one who spilled it."

"You?"

"I told him the truth about our moving Wilde's body."

She gasped. "Violetta, you didn't! I thought you were never going to tell anybody what we did. I'm sure we're in trouble now. What made you tell him?"

I couldn't tell her that I, too, had looked into a pair of green eyes and had starting talking. I didn't want to reveal that I trusted Mick McGuire when I had only just met him and knew he was a cop. I had acted on impulse when we moved the body and I had acted on impulse when I revealed the truth.

"They had already figured out he had been moved. They could tell by his clothing and by the scuffs his shoes made on the floor," I said. "And there was blood on the carpet. And plaster dust. I guess I thought it would be better to tell the truth."

"Did that giant trick you?" she asked with a funny look on her face.

I turned as red as McGuire's hair. "Something like that," I said.

I went back to my office and sat there for a while trying to think. I called my mom at home and my dad at his restaurant and told them the news. They were both horrified and kept asking me over and over if I was all right. I didn't tell them about my stupid stunt this morning. They would have thought that I had lost my mind.

I couldn't work, I couldn't concentrate on anything. I wanted to go home and walk my dogs. Craving fresh air, I went over to a window behind the desk that had a sign in Gothic lettering that said "*Don't Open.*" I opened it and stuck out my head as far as it would go. Taking gulps of fresh air I fought down the urge to scream or cry. What was going to happen to us? Was the harmonious, peaceful sanctity of our library world going to be permanently ruined with murder?

Across Lake Shore Drive I could see Lake Michigan sparkling in the sunlight. The cool fall day was refreshing and the sugar maple trees glowed with brilliant crimson and golden leaves. Down below there were still police cars and vans lining the street at the side of the library. I watched a woman in a blue jumpsuit and gloves exit the building holding something that looked like a tray of food. When she stood underneath me, I almost fainted. In her gloved hands she was holding a tray of *kourabiedes,* Greek cookies my dad had made especially for the party.

Chapter Seven

Tell me what you eat and I'll tell you what you are.

-Brillat-Savarin

At three o'clock there was an announcement on the loudspeaker. "*The library is closing early today, effective immediately. Please return all reference materials and check out all books before 3:15.*" The voice was our head of security. He repeated the announcement every five minutes until the building was cleared of all patrons. I punched out at 3:27 with Scarlett and Hugo right behind me. We stood in the hallway looking at each other. *What now?*

"What now?" I asked.

"I feel like a drink," Hugo said.

"That's the most sensible thing I've heard all day," Scarlett said. "Come on."

She pulled me out of the building and down the street. Nestled under the el tracks was a little retro looking bar that many of us librarians frequented on Fridays. Inside was a vintage oak bar, imported from Ireland, a fine piece of work from the early Art Deco period. Its mammoth mirror reflected the faces of the bar's inhabitants. Today there were many librarians who had come to discuss the day's shocking events. Their faces as seen in the antique glass had a soft glow, both from the lights on the bar and the drinks in their hands.

I ordered wine for the three of us. We found an empty table and I sat down on the hard wooden chair gratefully. I wanted to talk to Scarlett more about our semi-secret but I couldn't talk about it in front of Hugo. I wished he would go to the bathroom or go hang around someone else. We sat quietly sipping our wine, listening to the conversations that swirled around us. The de Winters were sitting together in a corner. Roxanne had stopped crying but looked like hell. Mark looked triumphant. Librarians from Fine Arts and History sat together at a big round table. Glasses and bowls of popcorn sat on the table within easy reach of nervous hands. Some librarians from other floors drifted in and immediately wanted to know what had happened today. The bar was beginning to resemble a library convention and I sighed. Enough already with the library talk, I was ready to go home and walk my dogs.

Hugo jumped up and went to the bar. I looked at Scarlett. "Did they ask you anything more?"

"Your friend stopped me on the way out and told me he would be coming in to talk to me first thing tomorrow morning," she said. "Anything I should know, do or say?"

"I've messed it up enough," I said, "just tell him the truth."

"OK, boss," she said with a smile.

"You don't seem too worried about it," I said.

"Why should I?" she said. "We didn't do anything that bad. We just moved him a little, we didn't kill him." She took her ringing cell phone out of her purse. "Peter, where are you? We're at the Blue Oyster, waiting for you."

Hugo returned with three more glasses of Chardonnay. I was shocked to see we had all drained our first glass so quickly. *Bloody hell, we're all nervy today.*

How can we go back to work tomorrow like nothing happened?

"Thank you, Hugo," I said.

"You're welcome, Violetta," he said. He was beaming. "Isn't it amazing how tragedy seems to bring us closer together?"

Scarlett and I looked at each other and rolled our eyes. We didn't have a good answer to that one. Hugo seemed in heaven, sitting between his "two favorite librarians." He acted like he was at a cozy little wedding instead of the preamble to a funeral. I wanted to throw catalog cards at him instead of rice.

Peter Lancaster strode in, like a man sitting on the eye of a tornado. He went to the bar, drained a shot of whiskey quickly and then came to our table holding another shot and a beer.

"This has been a momentous day," he said and raised his glass to the room. "Ladies and gentlemen, a toast- a toast to the death of Hieronymus Wilde, that bastard! May he rest in peace- and hell!"

There were gasps and shocked whispers. Hugo and Scarlett sat frozen. I was disgusted at this typical display of emotion. I had grown up with dramatic Mediterranean types, so I was used to this kind of bullshit.

"Sit down!" I ordered, pulling on his tweed jacket. "You're making an ass of yourself, again!"

He sat down immediately and looked contrite. This is why I assumed he was not the murderer. He always caved in when pressed, as many big, blustery men do when confronted with their sophomoric behavior.

"Sorry, Violetta," he said and sat down as meekly as a puppy. "I can't help it, it's divine retribution, Wilde's death. He stole my idea, sold it for God knows how much and wouldn't let me in on the money, the patent or the glory. No wonder they think I killed him." He picked up his shot glass and drained it. Then he took a big gulp of beer. *Scarlett would have to put him to bed later.*

"Did the police imply that you were responsible for his accident?" I asked.

He jumped up and signaled for a waitress. "No, but I can tell what they're thinking. They could never understand how I truly feel. The fools, how could they know what it feels like to have your life's work stolen from you, wrenched from your soul, your mind, nay-kidnapped from your very being?"

I almost gave him a standing ovation, he was that good. He could have played *Othello.* I could see him wringing Desdemona's neck with big crocodile tears in his eyes.

Scarlett placed a placating hand on his arm. "Peter, you're making a scene," she said. "Sit down, dearest."

He sat down and buried his face in his hands. I was getting pretty tired of this by now and wanted to go home.

"I've got to go to the bathroom," I said and got up. I passed a man wearing a trench coat sitting alone at a table reading the New York Times. He had a beer in front of him but he wasn't drinking. Something about him reminded me of Philip Marlowe or Mike Hammer and I wondered if he was a private detective, sent there to spy on us. At the next table Mark de Winter was sitting alone, slouched over a martini. He's not my favorite person, too brooding and Heathcliff-like for me to feel a connection with, but I was curious.

"How are you doing, Mark?" I slid into the chair next to him.

"I'm doing fine, Violetta," he said sardonically. "Just great. And as soon as I can get Roxanne to forget that dead jackass, I'll be fantastic."

"Roxanne cared for Wilde you know, she cared for him deeply." I didn't want to use the L word, too dangerous.

He snorted into his olives. "Bull! He was just a convenient lay for her."

"Really? It went on for years."

"She was mesmerized by the man's *presence.* Personally, I think she did it to annoy me."

I nodded like I understood. *Oh man, did he have an ego. And a hell of an id.*

"Maybe you can get her back, now that she's free."

He smiled, like I had finally said something brilliant.

"As soon as this investigation is over I want Roxanne to take a cruise with me, around the world, if possible."

Librarians don't make that much money. "Come into some cash?"

He smiled but it was more of a malevolent grimace.

"Perhaps," he said. "I have prospects." He stuck his nose back into his martini and I got up and left him. Like I said before, the run silent, run deep type gets on my nerves. Why not just come out and say what you're thinking?

I walked into the ladies' room. Once inside, it took me a minute to adjust my eyes to the dim light. I was surprised to find Roxanne de Winter standing in front of the mirror, trying to fix her face. She had out a brush, a container of power, lipstick and an eyebrow pencil and there were crumpled tissues in the sink.

"Hi, Roxanne," I said cautiously. I wasn't used to seeing her in a less than flawless condition. "How are you feeling?"

Her blue eyes filled with tears. "Horrible, absolutely horrible. I still can't believe that Hieronymus is dead. Poor, dear man." She sniffled into a tissue.

"It is a shock," I murmured.

"Why don't they arrest Peter Lancaster? He's always hated Hieronymus. He was always stalking him and threatening him."

"Well, they need evidence," I muttered, but she wasn't really listening to me. She was absorbed in her perfect reflection.

"I shouldn't have come here today, but Mark insisted," she said, dabbing powder on her red nose. A speck of powder fell on her chic, slim fitting, grey wool suit. She quickly brushed it away. Perfect as ever. "I thought he was going to offer me some comfort, but instead, he's just gloating. It's terrible, Violetta, I knew Mark hated Hieronymus, but I didn't know how much." She shivered. "It's frightening all the emotions we conceal under our polite exteriors."

Who's polite? This crowd had been especially vicious lately.

"Maybe Mark did it," I said, throwing discretion to the winds. "He's always wanted you back."

She allowed a tiny smile to crease her perfectly lined lips. She liked being Guinevere. "I'm sure Mark wouldn't have the nerve."

"He challenged Wilde to a duel," I reminded her.

"And lost," she reminded me. "Hieronymus scarred his face. But that's not enough motive for murder."

Isn't it?

"Maybe not," I said, but personally I thought she was full of it.

She sighed. "God, I'm so tired."

Yes, it's tiring having men fight over you.

"Why don't you go home? Why not get a taxi and go home and rest? It's been a terrible day for you."

"I will go home," she stood up and pushed everything into her chic Grace Kelly Hermes handbag. That bag cost five grand and Hieronymus gave it to her as a present after he hit it big with his patent. "I will not allow Mark to browbeat me anymore."

She gave me a weepy smile, squared her shoulders and walked out of the bathroom. All she needed was a hat and a veil.

When I returned to my table, Roxanne was gone. So was Mark. I hope he didn't follow her home, but really, did I care? She had never been overly friendly to me, just coolly polite. And Mark was too single minded about his devotion, no- obsession to Roxanne to be much of a friend or colleague.

Scarlett, Peter and Hugo were still drinking and eating popcorn. Peter looked semi-wasted, Hugo a bit tipsy and Scarlett looked enthused as always except the glassiness of her eyes gave it away that she was getting ripped. Shock does strange things to people, I know, but I didn't want to stay and lament the passing of Wilde. I didn't sit down.

"I'm going home," I said. "I want to go walk the dogs and get some fresh air."

"Shall I come with you?" Hugo said eagerly. "Can I escort you home?"

"No thanks, Hugo, stay and finish your drink. I can make it home all right." The CTA Brown Line was across the street. Up one flight of stairs, wait for the train and I would be home in a half hour. Hugo lived near the Red Line but he always waited for me so we could ride the Brown Line together to Belmont and then he would get off and make the change to the other train. Such devotion was touching but today I wanted to be alone.

"Are you sure?" he was rising in his seat and I gently pushed him back down. He looked disappointed.

"Stay," I ordered. "I see Punch and Judy waving at you." Two cute, young librarians from History, part of Wilde's groupies. "I'm sure they need cheering up. Go finish your drink with them." Hugo brightened up at the idea. He loved to gossip even more than he loved *me,* and I was grateful for that.

"Goodbye, y'all," I said. I grabbed my cape and practically ran out of the bar.

I sat on the el train in a dream, thinking about the day. Wilde was dead, I had met the only man who had piqued my interest since Siegfried had died and I needed a vacation. I wanted to pack up my pooches in my lime green Beetle and run off somewhere quiet and beautiful. The trees were changing spectacularly this fall and I longed for a weekend in Galena or Door County or maybe a trip to see the covered bridges in Parke County, Indiana. But I had been asked not to leave town, hadn't I, by the bossy giant?

I walked the three blocks home quickly. I live in a Victorian house, built in 1897. It's old, charming and drafty. There is an oak staircase and original woodwork with carved flowers around the doorways. Much of the original plumbing still exists and it needs work. But Siegfried and I were happy here and we had planned to upgrade and rehab slowly, when we could afford it. Now I didn't know when I would be able to do it, if ever.

It was only 4:30- I had gotten home an hour early. It felt wonderful. As soon as I put my key in the lock the ritual began. Samson and Delilah, my two Bichons, were waiting behind the hall door. I said, "Hi guys!" and all hell broke loose. The barking, the yipping, the leaping up to reach me, you'd think they hadn't seen me in nine years instead of nine hours. My mom comes over every day at 11 to let them out and play and I have a dog walker who comes every afternoon at 2:30. So they're well cared for but still you'd think I'd been gone forever.

We did our kisses and hugs and I passed out treats. They sat on the dining room carpet and waited expectantly. "OK, Samson and Delilah, just a minute." They wanted to walk. I drank a glass of water quickly and brushed my teeth because the wine had dried out my mouth. I had a bad taste at the back of my throat, probably from the coffee and donut and the pizza that had been brought in for us at noon. My healthy diet had gone to pieces today as well as my peace of mind.

I got the pups' leashes, and they jumped up. They were ecstatic with the thrill of taking a walk with me. Outside, I kept taking deep breaths of cool, crisp air. We walked down my quiet street to Waveland Avenue and then over along Ravenswood by the train tracks. I have always found the sound of trains comforting. I needed a lot of comfort today.

Wilde's death had been totally mind-blowing and disturbing. I kept thinking about Siegfried. He had complained of a backache five years ago and finally went to the doctor when I insisted. It had been stage 4 liver cancer and he had been dead six weeks later. I have never known such grief and despair. I couldn't work for three months and had to be sedated for two. I didn't know how much sadness a human soul could contain.

I had acted very foolishly today and I felt ashamed. I should have left the body where we had found him. Once again, I had acted on impulse, and I hoped it would not get me into the trouble I deserved. But after losing Siegfried, I had sometimes done things recklessly. I just didn't give a damn.

I was unusually penitent tonight. When we returned from our walk, I fed the dogs and went to change my clothes. I walked into my lilac colored bedroom and stared at myself in the full-length mirror. I saw a tall woman with enormous dark eyes and light olive skin. I had too much hair and too little skirt. I changed into black leggings, a black Ramones t-shirt that had belonged to Siegfried and a pair of old, worn, black Birks, my house slippers. I braided my hair and let the long rope trail down my back.

I read the papers and watched the news. Every channel mentioned the death in the library today but they were only calling it an accident and that the police were making investigations. It could still be an accident, couldn't it? Maybe Wilde fell and hit his head when the party was over and somehow wandered into my department to die? What was wrong with that scenario? I could almost believe it but there were too many people who hated Wilde. Someone had hit him over the head and had had left him to die or had left him in a totally fragile and feeble state.

I got hungry around eight o'clock and warmed up a bowl of *avgolemono* soup that my dad had made. Fragrant egg-lemon soup with rice with a nice toasty piece of Greek bread, covered in sesame seeds, was very soothing. I ate a piece of feta cheese, some black olives and took out the grapes. My pets waited expectantly for me to start feeding them as a treat and a game. I was idly sipping soup and rolling grapes on the dining room floor when the doorbell rang.

I did not often get evening visitors, so I expected to see someone selling something at the door. Usually I lift the lace curtain covering the glass and call out, "sorry, I'm busy!" but tonight it was no young solicitor, clipboard in hand, trying to wheedle donations out of the neighborhood. Tonight, my visitor wanted to wheedle something out of me.

Mick McGuire was standing on the front porch. I saw his red hair glowing in the porch light. I dropped the curtain and tried to step back quickly but of course he had already spotted me.

"Miss Aristotle," he said. "Violetta? Can I come in?"

I did not want him in my home, *our* home, but I had no choice but to open the door. Even though McGuire was attractive and appeared to have that dry sense of humor that I found very amusing, he was still a cop and I was still under suspicion.

I opened the door and pushed two white fluffy heads back. "Samson, Delilah! Stay inside!" I grabbed two collars with two fingers of one hand and opened the storm door with the other. "Come in, quickly, before they go crazy." They loved company.

McGuire stepped inside and even though my front hall has a high ceiling of about 11 feet, he seemed to fill up every inch of space in it. I stood in the hall silently. My dogs circled him happily, jumping up, waiting to be petted. McGuire complied with their wishes and scratched their necks while they responded affectionately. My pooches like to be admired and adored.

"Stop it, enough," I finally said. "They'll keep this up all night if you let them."

He dropped his hands. "Cute dogs, my grandmother had a Bichon Frise when I was growing up. Sweet animals."

Amazing, he knows what a Bichon Frise is. Most people don't.

What is she wearing? All in black- glowing, gorgeous, a punk Morticia. No mini-skirts tonight. The Ramones, I see. Amazing.

"Can I help you with something?" I asked in my best reference room voice.

He looked into the dining room. He saw plates and the candles I always lit when I had a meal. "I've disturbed your dinner," he said. "And you probably have company."

"It's OK, I'm finished. And I ate alone." I heaved a sigh. "Come on in."

He followed me inside. I saw him quickly take in the pumpkin colored walls, the framed vintage posters of Elvis, Josephine Baker and Maurice Chevalier and the Chinese deco rugs that covered the hardwood floors. Most of them I had bought at auctions or on eBay, a solace to me in the years that had followed my husband's death.

"Nice home," he said. "Colorful." He was staring at the hot pink walls in my office and piano room.

"I like color, it makes me happy," I said.

"Like your pink shoes today?"

I stared at him coolly. "Did you come here to talk about my shoes or was it something important?"

He was staring at my bowl of soup.

"That smells delicious," he said. "What is it?"

"Greek soup," I said and then gave up. "Would you like to try some?"

His face lit up like a little boy. "I would love some."

I went into the kitchen and heated up more soup. I toasted bread and made up a plate of cheese, grapes and olives. I put on the tea kettle. Greeks and Italians like to eat and when you come into our homes we want to feed you. Even if we don't like you, it's in our nature to stuff you full of life affirming food. He followed me.

"Would you like a beer? A glass of wine?

"No thanks, a glass of water would be great."

I paused, reaching for a glass. "Still on duty?"

"Yes, I am."

"So this isn't a social call."

He smiled. "I wish it was."

I felt my stomach lurch. *Too many olives? Did he have a warrant for my arrest?* I put his food on a tray which he immediately took from my hands. He waited politely.

"Let's sit in the dining room," I said.

Wasn't this cozy, me and the giant and Samson and Delilah eating a little *avgolemono* on a chilly, autumn evening? I shut my eyes for a second and tried to remember the nights me and Siegfried had done just this, a little food, laughter, love and conversation. It seemed a million years ago.

We sat down and he immediately starting eating. He didn't talk and neither did I. After a few spoonfuls of soup and some mouthfuls of bread and cheese, he looked at me and grinned.

"This is delicious. I'm sorry I'm just eating without talking, but I was starving."

"I can see that," I smiled back. "Do you like the soup?"

"Absolutely, what's it called?"

"*Avgolemono*, it means egg and lemon."

"Did you make it?"

"No, my dad does. He's a chef, he owns a restaurant downtown."

"What's the name of it?"

"Sam's Place, it's down by the opera house, on Wacker Drive."

"I know that restaurant; I've eaten many an early morning omelet there."

"Then you've probably seen my dad, he's the tall, dark man who's always running around in the middle of everything and everybody."

"I've seen him; he looks like a really great guy. And what a great place to eat."

"Dad's worked hard there for 40 years. First he was a waiter when he came here from Greece and then a cook and then he bought out the original owner. He's there every morning at 5am and he closes up at 3pm. He's very dedicated to his business."

"Did he teach you to cook?"

"I can cook a little," I admitted. "Not as good as him, though. My mother is a great cook, too. You should taste her lasagna."

"I'd like to," he said. "Anytime you say."

I ignored that and took a sip of tea.

He finished the soup and picked off a few grapes. The dogs sat by his side, waiting.

"It's OK?" he asked.

"OK," I said and he held out a grape to each dog. They took them in their teeth and trotted off to play.

"Want some more?" I asked.

"No, that will hold me for a while. Thanks."

"Didn't you eat, today?"

"When I get a new case, I get too keyed up to eat. I get so into it."

I wonder if he gets into his love affairs with the same enthusiasm.

I haven't had dinner fixed for me by a woman since my divorce, two years ago. And she's so beautiful. I could get used to this.

"Speaking of cases, anything new about Wilde?"

He looked at me oddly, and I felt my heart plummet.

"As a matter of fact, there is."

"Yes?" I felt myself grow hot then cold. Would he say anything about the Greek cookies I saw being removed by the crime lab?

He let out some air like a silent whistle and looked at me closely.

"Hieronymus Wilde was not killed by falling or by the blow to his skull," he said quietly. "He was killed by poison. Arsenic."

I almost fell off my chair. I gripped the sides with both hands to keep from going into a full scale Greco-Roman tizzy.

"Arsenic?" I said. "How could that be? How did he get arsenic?"

He looked at me again. "You're not going to like this, Violetta, but arsenic was found in a tray of cookies hidden in the back of your department. The cookies, which were covered in powdered sugar, were covered with arsenic."

I swallowed, once, twice and then jumped up. "I've got to go to the bathroom." I couldn't breathe and ran the water very loudly while I did my business and splashed cool water on my burning cheeks.

When I came out McGuire was sitting in the living room, playing with the dogs. He looked comfortable sitting on my overstuffed leopard print sofa. He looked right at home.

"Composed now?" he asked pleasantly. "Have you thought of a good story as to why your dad's cookies were covered in arsenic?"

Chapter Eight

I'm trying to think, but nothing happens.

-Curly Howard, Three Stooges

It was after 8 o'clock and I was starting to get tired. I'm afraid I let all my good intentions evaporate and really let him have it.

"What do you mean?" I demanded. "How should I know why Pop's cookies had arsenic on them? That's your job, and what the hell are you implying? My father made 10 trays of *kourabiedes* and every one of them was absolutely perfect when they left the restaurant! How would I know how some perverted murderer stole the tray and put poison on them? And why weren't we all poisoned? We all ate some! And another thing," I was pulling apart my braid in extreme agitation, "what do you mean, have I thought of a good story? If you think I have something to do with this, then just arrest me and let's get this the hell over with!" My voice had risen in a crescendo of anger. My face was twisted like a Kabuki mask. My dogs sat and looked at me, their little heads cocked to one side. They hadn't seen me this pissed since they chewed up my blue suede Elvis shoes I bought at Lansky's in Memphis.

"Beautiful," he said quietly. "Truly beautiful."

"What?" I asked, hands on hips. I was not amused or appeased by his manner.

"You're really beautiful when you're angry."

"And why shouldn't I be angry?" I fumed. "You're accusing my father of murdering Wilde!"

"Now wait a minute, I'm not accusing him of anything. I am just giving you the facts. Greek cookies covered in arsenic, Wilde dies of arsenic poisoning, your father made the cookies- you do the math. And I'm not accusing you. It's just kind of funny that when someone asks you a very direct question, you go stick chopsticks in your hair or go to the bathroom."

"Why shouldn't I go to the bathroom? Is there some kind of law against that?"

"Now calm down," he said.

"I am calm, and you just keep your comments about how I look to yourself!" I said, getting more and more worked up. "It's unprofessional to talk about my hair or skirt or tell me I'm pretty."

"I said beautiful," he said and got off the sofa.

I backed away. I'm a tall, strong woman, but he was way too big for me to handle.

He kept coming until we both stopped in the middle of the dining room. He was only inches away and I was staring at his cleft chin and trying not to think totally impure thoughts.

"You smell like lemons," he said. I ignored that. "I'm sorry I offended you, I'll try and keep it very professional from now on."

"I'm sorry I yelled at you," I said. "I know you're only doing your job, as they say." I raised my eyebrows. "You smell like limes."

He ignored that. "Any ideas?"

"I think we should go talk to my dad," I said. "Maybe he can help you out."

"I was hoping you'd say that," he said.

"You were?"

"I came here tonight to tell you about Wilde and the arsenic because I knew you would be able to tell me about the cookies- how do you pronounce them?"

"Koo-ra-bee-eth-es," I sounded out.

"Kour-a-bessie," he repeated.

"Close enough," I said. "koura- byie, thes-"

"Kourabiedes," he said perfectly.

"*Opaa*," I said, "we'll make a Greek out of you, yet."

"What does *opaa* really mean?"

"It means hurray and wow and good luck and all that good stuff," I told him. "It's kind of an untranslatable Greek word for very good things."

"You're kind of like that, Violetta," he said softly, "You make me feel happy when I'm around you."

Zing. I gave him the eye.

"Sorry," he said.

"Professionalism, remember?" I reminded him. "I'm not going to get angry and you are going to act professionally. Don't you have a girlfriend or a wife to flirt with?"

Smooth, Violetta, really cool girl.

"I've been divorced for two years," he said. "I live a quiet life."

I would think women would chase you down the street.

"I would think women would chase you down the street," I blurted out.

He smiled. "Hardly," he said wryly. "I've been told by one Match.com woman that I resembled a red-headed Frankenstein. Also Alfred E. Neuman from Mad Magazine. And another said she wouldn't want to go out with a man who had to wear a gun and who looked like a dead president."

"Which president?" I said, "Millard Fillmore?"

"Funny," he said. I felt the mood change dramatically. I liked this man and I knew he was not going to persecute me or my family.

I went to the front hall to get the leashes and my cape. "I'm sure a few Match.com ladies liked what they saw."

"A few," he admitted, "but we didn't click. And I work odd hours."

He took the cape from my hands and held it out for me. I slipped into it effortlessly, like Sabrina dashing out with Humphrey Bogart.

"Ready?" I asked.

We walked the 10 minutes to my parents' home. The evening air was cool and refreshing and we didn't hurry. The only sound was the tip tap of the dog's nails as they hit the sidewalks.

"Why did you get divorced?" I asked.

"She didn't want to have kids."

"For real?" *Who wouldn't want at least one little bambino?*

"For real," he said. "Or at least she didn't want to have kids with me."

I let this alone for a minute. It could still be bothering him.

"I would think you'd make an excellent father," I said carefully.

"Thank you for that, Violetta," he said.

We walked in silence the rest of the way, stopping once to talk to Flo, a neighborhood dog, who my babies adored. She was a collie with a lot of love in her heart and a sweet demeanor. She was a lady, if you know what I mean. My mother who is a tender 55 years young and who went to school in the days of panty girdles and white gloves has been known to say to me, "Violetta, men like ladies," many times since I hit puberty until I was ready to puke.

"You've been a widow how long?" his gentle, deep voice broke into my thoughts.

"Five years," I said.

"Big Fat Greek Wedding?" he asked.

"No," I said, "the exact opposite. I think my parents were shocked when I ran off to marry Siegfried at City Hall. Also broken hearted. They would have liked the big wedding, with all the relatives and the big accordion-bouzouki band."

"Any brothers and sisters?"

"No, I'm an only child."

"So that's why your folks are broken hearted. They wanted a big wedding."

"Well, I've been a disappointment so far. No big wedding, no grandchildren, no prospects of either."

"It ain't over 'til it's over," he quoted softly.

I couldn't think of a snappy comeback and we were in front of my parents' house. Although it was a cool night my father was a fresh air freak and the living room windows were open. From inside the house we could hear my mother singing "Mon coeur s'ouvre a ta voix," from Saint Saens' opera, Samson and Delilah. Through the curtains blowing in the breeze I saw the great silver candelabra lit and my father sitting raptly listening while my mother sang and play. I was sure I had interrupted a romantic evening for them and I hated myself for that. I walked up to the front door and hesitated, my hand hovering over the door bell. A strong hand caught mine.

"Wait," he said, "wait until she stops singing. Don't wreck the moment."

I looked up at him in shock. A cop with the soul of an artist. *Mamma mia!*

We stood listening to Delilah sing of her love for Samson, (while eyeing his hair) and I felt like crying. That such beauty could exist on such an amazing fall night, after such an extraordinarily fantastic and terrible fall day warmed my heart. My companion also stood rooted, listening to my mother's lush, ripe contralto.

Who could not respond to the beauty of the words, *my heart opens at the sound of your voice, like the flowers in the morning sun?* And later- *shower on me, your tender words, your raptures?* We both stood transfixed as if we had heard of love for the first time. My dogs, accustomed to hearing their grandma's singing, stood patiently and respectfully. I looked at Mick McGuire and wondered what planet he had wandered in from. He was humming along with my mother. A policeman that knew Camille Saint-Saens?

Was he a Martian? Immediately I felt contrite. I was becoming hard and jaded. Why shouldn't he know opera? Why shouldn't he have a refined soul? I had been a widow too long and was becoming as brittle as the spine of an original Huck Finn, published in 1884. I was becoming a vintage spinster, and I hated it.

My mother finished the aria and both my dad and McGuire burst into applause.

"Bravo, bravo," they both shouted. I stood frozen and blinked back tears. The dogs started barking. My father opened the front door.

"No applause, just money," he said. Pop does like his old jokes. When he was an immigrant in the 60's he learned English by watching the *Dick Van Dyke Show* and *Laugh In*. He still likes to say "sock it to me, baby." And when *Kojak* with Telly Savalas came out in the seventies, Pop was on Mount Olympus. He passed out lollipops for years at the restaurant.

"Dad, I'm sorry to drop in like this," I said formally.

My father looked at me like I was crazy. Drop in? I always dropped in, anytime day or night. I rolled my eyes and nodded my head in the direction of the giant behind me.

"Come in, welcome," he said to McGuire. "Any friend of Violetta's is a friend of mine."

"Thank you, sir," said Mick.

"I'm Sam Aristotle," said my dad, extending a strong hand.

"I'm Mick McGuire," he answered, taking Pop's hand in his strong grasp. "Chicago Police Department."

Chapter Nine

Insanity runs in my family. It practically gallops.

-Mortimer Brewster, Arsenic and Old Lace

My father acted like he didn't hear him and kept shaking his hand.

"Sophia-" my dad shouted into the living room. "Come here and meet a friend of Violetta's!"

My beautiful petite dark haired mother entered the hallway. She was a 5'2 dynamo of activity with a voice and a face to die for. No wonder Pop fell for her like a ton of bricks when she came into the restaurant 35 years ago after a rehearsal at the Lyric Opera.

"Why are you shouting?" she asked. "And why are we standing in the hall? Come in."

We came in. My dogs acted like they hadn't seen my parents in a million years. They jumped up and barked and were as happy as can be because they were with their favorite humans on the planet.

"I'm Sophia Aristotle," my mother said to Mick, extending a small, delicate white hand.

He took her hand and practically bowed over it. "I'm so happy to meet you; your daughter looks just like you."

"We do look alike," Sophia said. "It's been such a joy for me to have my only child resemble her parents."

"Yes, I've got Pop's height and Mom's hair," I said. "She's the pretty one of us two." I love my Mother, she's really a peach.

"I think you've got her looks, too," McGuire said softly.

There was a silence for a second and then we all burst into speech.

"Mom and Dad, Mick is here from the Police Department to ask about-"

"Would you like something to drink?" my mother asked.

"Now what's this I hear about you being with the police?" My dad said. "It's a shame that-"

"I loved hearing you sing, Mrs. Aristotle," Mick said. "My grandmother-"

We all stopped and laughed. We were ready for Comedy Central.

"Sit down," my mother urged, steering Mick into the biggest armchair in the room, usually reserved for my father. "I'm going to make some coffee."

McGuire looked around at the room decorated in sleek black and white modern furniture. The focal point of the room was the white grand piano which made a striking contrast to my mother's black hair and eyes.

"This is a beautiful room," he said.

My mother smiled. She loves compliments and takes them well, unlike her daughter.

He then took his official badge out of his pocket. "I've got to show you this." Both my parents stared at the badge without comment.

"I'll start the coffee," my mother said. She hurried off into the kitchen and I went to help her.

"So, you bring a tall, charming policeman here without telling me," she said immediately when the door was closed. "What's going on?"

"Ma- he's just investigating Wilde's death."

"At this hour?"

"He had some bad news and I think he should tell you about it himself."

She fiddled with the coffee maker and a plate of desserts without speaking. When my parents are preparing food they are not interested in anything else. The food was the goal and the goal was to please.

We returned to the living room together.

"Just a couple more minutes," my mother said, "and we'll have some nice, hot coffee and cake. It's gotten chilly tonight."

My dad was sitting looking bemused. My mother zoned in on that immediately.

"What's the matter? Has something happened?" she asked anxiously. "Nobody has been bothering Violetta?"

Mick took a breath and my father rushed in. You can't beat a Greek when he's ready to talk.

"Something unbelievable has happened." He made the sign of the cross and grabbed the gold crucifix he always wore around his neck. "Mr. Wilde was poisoned by arsenic that they found in my *kourabiedes.*" Dad's voice dropped an octave. "And he-" he pointed at Mick, "wants to know if I know anything." Dad looked stumped and turned to his lifelong partner for assistance. "Do I? Do I know anything, Sophia?"

My mother has a very cool head in times of trouble, she's not like my dad or me, who tend to ramble on and get hysterical. She looked at my "friend," and said, "Could you tell us what happened?"

Mick took his BlackBerry and began punching buttons.

"Mr. Wilde was found in the History department this morning approximately at 7:30am. He had a bump on his head. Our first thought was he had died from a fall and head injuries. There was an autopsy conducted today and it was discovered that Mr. Wilde had a lethal dose of arsenic in his system. He was poisoned first and then hit on the head. A tray of *kourabiedes* was found in the Reference and Reading Room, hidden under a revolving dictionary stand. Some of the cookies had been liberally covered in powdered arsenic.

"How many?" my mother asked.

Mick looked apologetic. "I'm not at liberty to say."

Wow. Cops really do talk like that. I felt like I was in the middle of a Hawaii Five-0 rerun.

"So you'd like to know when we made the cookies and how they got to the library?"

My mom always has a grasp on the essentials. A timer went off in the kitchen.

"Coffee's ready," she said.

Mick jumped up. "Let me help you, Mrs. Aristotle."

My mother always has an eye for an attractive, masculine man.

"Thank you," she said, "how kind of you."

"And I wanted to tell you how much I enjoyed your singing," Mick said. "My grandmother listened to the Met broadcasts from New York every Saturday on the radio when I was a kid, and I heard a lot of opera. You have a beautiful voice."

"Thank you," said my mother. She was beaming. I knew she would Google him tonight.

They went into the kitchen and my dad looked at me with big, wide eyes.

"So now I'm a mass murderer," he said.

"Dad, only one man is dead," I said.

"Yes," he said, his voice rising in frustration, "but after eating my *kourabiedes*! What the hell goes on there in your library? Who would fool around with my food? This is terrible-" he made the evil eye sign with his hand; a real tip off he was upset. He looked at me carefully. "Are you in trouble?"

I felt like I was five years old again. I sighed. "No, Pop, I'm not in trouble." Not yet. Thank God, he hadn't told them about me and Scarlett moving Wilde's body.

My mother and Mick came back into the living room carrying trays. He had the coffee pot and cups and my mother was holding a crystal platter covered in pastries, cookies and nougat candies.

"Mick insisted on trying these," she said, pointing to a few *kourabiedes*. She picked up a plate and put some of the notorious cookies on a plate along with a piece of *karithopita.* "Violetta, *koukla mou*, how about a piece of cake? I just made it tonight, it's still warm." I knew she had made the honey-nut cake for her book club tomorrow but had cut it for the arrival of the red-haired one. I also knew she would stay up past midnight making another. I stuck out my tongue at her. She responded in kind. Mick stared at us with interest.

"Ignore them," said my father, "they're like children when they get together."

"I can see that," Mick said and smiled at us. *My, weren't we cozy?*

Samson and Delilah sat patiently waiting for a crumb to fall. My mother had brought in the dog chews and they each got one as a bribe to be good. My mother poured coffee and passed it all around. Mick took a sip and then picked up a *kourabiedes* off his plate. We all held our breaths. He took a bite and nodded his head.

"This is delicious," he said. "What is that spice?" He sniffed a bit and took another bite. "Cinnamon? No, cloves, I think."

"Correct," my father beamed at him. "You've got a good nose."

"It's part of my work," Mick said and smiled. "Thank you for the lovely desserts, Mrs. Aristotle. It's been a real Greek night. First, your daughter gives me *avgolemono* soup and now I get *kourabiedes.*" He pronounced the words perfectly. My mother and father gave each other the *look.* I'd have a lot of explaining to do later.

"We are so happy to meet Violetta's friends," my mother said. "Sometimes I think she spends too much time with-" she dropped her voice a few dulcet tones, "librarians."

"Heavens forbid," I said and choked on my coffee. Mick tried not to laugh. I caught his eye, and God help me, I felt I was falling madly in love.

We ate for a while in companionable silence. I threw toys to the dogs and they caught them and brought them back to us. My mother sat humming a bit of an aria and my dad sat looking at my mother. God, they were happy. Although they had been so nice to Siegfried they had never really understood him and he had never been entirely comfortable with their all-encompassing love and affection. He had felt more comfortable with his books.

"I hate to bring this up but could you please tell me when you made the cookies that went to the party last night?" Mick asked after finishing the cake and three *kourabiedes.*

"I made them yesterday morning, so they would be fresh and nice for the party," my dad explained.

McGuire had picked up his phone and was typing into it. My mother and father gave each other the look again.

"Did anyone else help you make the *kourabiedes*?"

"My cook, Stavros- Steve helped me, you know that Sophia, he's good with the baking," my dad said.

"Of course, Stavros has a good hand with pastry dough and cakes, a very light touch," she agreed.

"Anyone else help you?"

"No, no one," Sam said.

"Do you remember if any librarians came in for lunch yesterday?"

That one I hadn't thought of. My dad frowned and thought for a bit.

"You'd have to ask my hostess, she would remember better than me. I'm so busy with the cooking and customers I wouldn't be able to tell you"

"Of course," Mick agreed. "Her name?"

"Dorothy Frye," Pop said.

"Is she Greek?"

"No, she married the son of one of my cousins," he said. "Nice girl."

I thought of this "nice girl" and then thought of Mick interviewing her. She was looking for her third husband at 40 and I didn't trust her one inch with a good looking man. She would vamp him and stick out her enormous silicone bosoms and give him the real once over. *Why was I feeling jealous?*

"Do you have to interview her?" I asked.

"Someone will," Mick said quietly. He was still typing away. "Who took the tray of cookies over to the library?"

"I think Gus did. He's one of the waiters and he does pick-ups and deliveries for me. Are you getting all that? Do you want me to talk slower?" My dad asked Mick.

"No, that's fine, I got it."

Sam smiled. "Good, I don't want you to miss anything. Everything I say is of earth shattering importance."

My mother and I laughed. This was an old joke. Mick looked up startled.

"You all get along very well," he said.

"Don't you get along with your family?" I asked.

"My mom and dad are both gone. I lived with my grandmother for many years. She's a wonderful woman but I missed some of your camaraderie. It looks like you all have fun."

"We have a good time," my father said. "I'm sorry for your loss."

"My mom died of cancer when I was 8 and my dad died in a car crash when I was 11. It was unbelievable. My grandma kept my brother and me from losing it when we were kids and kept us out of trouble when we were older. We were real hell raisers, pardon my language," he added, with a look at my mother.

"Of course, I understand completely," she said, and she did.

"So, it's been great to meet you and thank you for inviting me into your home after I intruded without warning," Mick said. "I should get back downtown. If you think of anything else - you will call me?" Mick took out a card and handed it to my dad.

"Of course, I will, right away, no problem," he said. He stood up and shook his hand again.

"I'll see you tomorrow," Mick said to my father.

He took my mother's small white hand in his huge strong one and shook it gently.

She smiled up at him. "You're very sweet," she said.

"Thank you for your hospitality," he said. "I'm going to walk Violetta home now."

I got the leashes for my pooches and my cape. Once again he held it out for me. I felt his warmth through the velvet-lined wool cape. I shivered.

"Cold?" he murmured.

"Yes," I said, but in reality I was burning up.

After many warm farewells and the promise to return we hit the street. We walked home quickly and without a lot of chat.

"I like your parents," he said.

"Thanks. They're really special."

"Your mother has a beautiful voice."

"She sang quite a few roles at the Lyric Opera. She still gets cards and flowers from her fans on her birthday. She is always amazed by the attention."

"You're an amazing family," he said.

At the door I stuck out my hand formally. "Thanks for being so nice to Mom and Pop. He didn't look it, but he was really upset about the *kourabiedes* having poison on them. That's the worst thing that can happen to a Greek, having their food contaminated."

"I can understand that," he towered over me in the darkness. I kept staring up at him. The dogs started scratching at the door. I woke up out of my trance and took out my keys. I opened the door. He leaned in close and I held my breath. But he only pushed the door for me and the pooches scampered inside.

"Goodnight," I said, "will you be at the library tomorrow?"

"Yes," he said, "I'll be there. See you then." He gave me a small, inscrutable smile and walked down the front steps. At the bottom he turned around. "Violetta-"

"Yes?"

"Please don't say anything about how Wilde died to your friends. We're going to fill them in on the facts tomorrow." His tone of voice was not a request.

"Of course, I understand," I said, crossing my fingers behind my back. He nodded and walked away.

Inside I looked at myself in the mirror. He hadn't mentioned dinner or a drink or the famous, "let's have coffee." Maybe I was reading too much into his behavior. Maybe all this personal attention was just to get me to relax and to open up and talk.

I felt like Cupid had shot me with his bow and arrow and I felt foolish. I didn't want to fall in love with a cop; I still loved Siegfried, didn't I? I was still the un-Merry Widow, pining away for a lost love. Having a crush on McGuire, however tall and intelligent he seemed, would be inconvenient. I'd have to change my routine.

The phone message light was blinking. It was Corny calling in behalf of Mrs. Vandermeer.

"There is an emergency meeting tomorrow at 8:30 in the auditorium," he said, "at the request of Mrs. Vandermeer. Please be there."

So we had to show up half an hour early, without pay, to hear her read us the riot act about the unsavory goings on at the Midwestern University Library. And I supposed McGuire would be in the shadows making notes on his BlackBerry.

I took a deep breath, wrestled with my finer instincts and then picked up the phone and called Scarlett.

Chapter Ten

The Sword of Damocles

-ancient legend

After a very restless night, I got up early and walked the dogs. Twice. Then I trotted off to the el and got downtown before 8 o'clock. After I signed in with security and swiped in I went to the cafeteria for tea and toast. I didn't feel like walking into my department alone today. I didn't feel like walking into my department at all.

Many librarians had my idea and were drinking coffee and talking. There was an air of expectancy in their hushed voices. They were all expecting some revelation to fall from the southern fried lips of our director, Mrs. Vandermeer.

I wasn't expecting anything more than a chastisement motivated by politics and her desire to leave for Washington, D.C. She was going to blame us for Wilde's death and probably insist the murderer get up and turn himself in ***immediately***. *If it were only that easy.*

I sat with the oldest living librarian in captivity, Jerry Schwegel from Literature. I swear to God he used to eat lunch with Proust. He taught Peter Lancaster how to play the bagpipes and they still go to this convention once a year, wear kilts and hang out with other bagpipe *aficionados.* Like I said before, librarians are a colorful group.

I saw Scarlett and Peter talking to Roxanne across the room but I didn't want to be near my assistant right now. I was afraid she had already told Peter about the arsenic. I was feeling badly that I hadn't kept McGuire's confidence.

"When is the wake for Wilde?" the old guy asked me.

"I don't know," I said. "I heard Dolly's sisters came up from Savannah last night and they haven't made any plans yet. But they're talking about something big."

"Well, they can't wait around forever," he chortled, "he won't keep fresh indefinitely."

"You're really a scream, Jerry," I said and put down my toast. My appetite had left me. "I imagine they have to wait for the police to release the body."

"Oh, yes, the autopsy," he said and tugged his grizzled mustache in anticipation. I felt guilty again. I hoped Scarlett hadn't talked. Or, and this thought struck me as unpleasant, maybe McGuire had wanted me to talk? Then he could observe everyone's reaction. Maybe his interest in me was just a ruse and his coming over last night had been a devious attempt to get me to spill it. I felt confused.

At 8:25 there was a mass exodus from the cafeteria. I cleaned off my tray and followed the lambs to the slaughter. Today I was very tastefully attired in another black cashmere sweater and the longest black skirt I could find in my closet. It was vintage black crepe from the 40's and was trimmed with a couple of rows of small black ruffles. It skimmed my ankles and I felt like I was ready for the convent. I wore plain black pantyhose and my hair was arranged in a very prim bun at the nape of my neck. Today of all days, I didn't want to be conspicuous.

We all filed into the auditorium and took our seats. On the stage stood Lois Dalton Vandermeer, her assistant Cornell Hamilton, two men in suits and Mick McGuire. I felt a jolt when I looked at him. I was seated near the back and yet I found his eyes were upon me immediately.

Scarlett dropped into the seat next to me and looked wild with excitement.

"I hope you didn't say anything to Peter," I said to her in a low voice.

"Of course I didn't! I couldn't anyway because Peter was passed out by the time you called and I went home to my own apartment afterwards."

Thank God for that.

"Thank God for that," I said, getting worked up. "I never should have told you in the first place. What was the matter with me? I wasn't supposed to tell anybody."

"*He*," she nodded at the giant on stage, "asked you to keep it a secret and you did. You only told me, and I don't count."

"No?" I asked her skeptically. "Why not?"

"Because I'm your assistant and because I helped you move you know who," she said. "So we're in this together."

Yes, but how far were we in it?

There were no bells rung this morning. Only the snapping on of the microphone and the cold, steely voice of our fearless leader silenced our whispers.

"I called you all here early this morning because Detective McGuire has something to tell you," Mrs. Vandermeer said. She was part southern belle this morning, part society maven.

"Union contract," someone said from the audience. Mrs. Vandermeer wrinkled her nose and started tapping her toe on the stage. We had a couple of staunch union reps in our midst. They would try and get us out a half hour early to make up for this morning. She opened her mouth to speak and then snapped it shut. I waited for her to explode like Krakatoa.

Instead she passed the microphone to McGuire and went and took a seat. I held my breath and found I was sweating. Next to me Scarlett was clenching her hands. The tension in the room was so thick you could body surf on it.

"Ladies and gentlemen," he began, "good morning. I'm sorry to have to get you here so early this morning. Please think of your being here without compensation as part of your duty as a good citizen." A few snickers broke out in the back of the room. I hope they wouldn't boo or hiss. Did I mention librarians are notorious rabble-rousers? We love a good fight.

"We have some information about Mr. Hieronymus Wilde's death. It was not accidental, it was murder."

Gasps went around the room. One very nervous librarian from Philosophy screamed. The History groupies cried as one, "oh no!" and two burst into tears. Peter Lancaster patted Roxanne's hand. Mark wasn't around for this; maybe he had started his world tour. Dolly Wilde was naturally at home grieving. Or was she? Maybe she had gotten out the red dress and the castanets to celebrate.

"Does Dolly know?" Scarlett poked me in the ribs.

"Ouch," I rubbed my side. "I don't know. I imagine the great one has been over there to tell her." The great one raised his hands and silenced the crowd.

"Neat trick," Scarlett whispered. I choked back a laugh. I think I was getting hysterical.

"What was the cause of death?" Hugo called out in his best crime lab voice.

"Death by arsenic poisoning," McGuire said. Pandemonium ensued. This time the three librarians from serials cataloging screamed and Roxanne de Winter fainted. By the time she was revived and helped out of room the crowd had quieted down and I was exhausted.

"I'm sorry to upset you," he continued at last, "but you must realize that everyone here must be questioned again."

"Are we suspects?" Hugo asked. He was sitting between Punch and Judy. They were looking at him adoringly, like he was their protector. He really did have an adorable profile.

"At this moment in time, no one is a special suspect, but everyone at the party needs to questioned," he answered. "I hope I can stress the fact that anything you saw or heard last night is of the utmost importance. I want you all to think about where you were seated and what went on during the party."

"Like what?" asked Hugo.

"Can you remember who Wilde was talking to, what he was eating and anything else that could help us," McGuire said. "Did he have an argument with anyone and did he get his own food or did someone bring it to him?"

A groupie raised her hand.

"Yes, Miss?"

"Dolly Wilde and Miss Aristotle brought him his food," she said. She turned to me with a teary face. "Remember? Mrs. Wilde had plates of food and cheese and you were carrying the plates with those powdered cookies on them," she said.

I nodded my head. Great, I had just admitted to serving Wilde the poisoned *kourabiedes.* I looked at McGuire and he looked at me. He was not amused. Hell, neither was I. At this rate the entire Aristotle clan would be behind bars before long. Dad imprisoned for making the stuff and me for serving it. It was a conspiracy, probably planned by the Turks, as my grandmother used to say.

"We'll look into it, Miss." McGuire said. "This is purely voluntary at this moment in time but if you agree we would like to take your fingerprints." A ripple of protest went around the room. "As I said it's voluntary, right now, but it would help speed up our investigation. When we come to your departments this morning, we can take your prints then."

I looked at Scarlett. I'm sure this was because of Wilde's walking stick and the wiped off prints. She had the grace to blush. I shook my head in resignation.

"You can go back to your departments now, we will be around to talk to all of you and take your statements. Please try to remember if you saw anything unusual that night," he said. He looked at Mrs. Vandermeer. "Thank you, ma'am. I'm through for now."

She stood up and took the microphone. We waited. "I will not be going to Washington this week," she said. "I will be staying on as director until this terrible tragedy is over." She looked furious. "I will be calling some of you into my office today to discuss matters. You may go now."

She was regal, I'll give her that. I would love to develop more of her attitude. I would love to have some of her millions, too, that would probably help me be more assertive.

We all got up and started off to our departments. It was 10 minutes to opening. I stopped at the mail room to get today's newspapers. Scarlett and I were the morning shift today and two junior librarians were working 10-6 and another two 12-8. Our library pages, all university students, would come in at 2 to shelve books and clean up. Tuesday mornings were usually fairly quiet and I welcomed the peace and the chance to work. I was behind on my book orders.

"I'm going to the ladies room," Scarlett said and left me at the escalator. I rode up to the third floor, unlocked the main doors to the Reference and Reading Room and walked to the circulation desk. This time I carefully walked behind the desk, half expecting to bump into another bag or body. The floor was pristine, the carpeting unsullied by any remains. I put away my coat and bags in my office. I walked past the book stacks. I wanted to get a book cart so I could clean out the old newspapers. I didn't feel like waiting for the library pages. I wanted to do some manual labor first before I sat down. Behind the last stack of reference books was the row of book carts. When I saw what was draped across the last metal book cart I dropped my sack of newspapers and tried to scream but my vocal chords were paralyzed.

The body of Mark de Winter was lying flat on his back across the cart. His throat was pierced with a fencing sword and he was absolutely stone cold dead. Blood poured down his neck, covering his white Irish fisherman's sweater and khaki pants. The floor was drenched in blood and there was an obscene dripping noise as Mark's body fluids hit the marble tiles. His eyes were frozen with a horrendous expression that I had only seen in old vampire flicks. I clutched my stomach and tried to breathe but the room was spinning. This time I had no childish notion to touch the body. This time I staggered to the phone on the circulation counter and dialed 911.

Within 55 seconds I heard voices and footsteps running down the hall. Mick McGuire and two detectives ran in the Reference Room. When they saw me, trying to hold myself up against the counter they ran up to me.

"Are you all right?" McGuire demanded.

I pointed to the rear of the book stacks. "Go- it's de Winter and he's dead!"

They left me and ran back. I heard a whistle, a curse and then nothing. After a few seconds McGuire walked up to the desk and found me still holding the counter for dear life. He lowered me into a chair and got out a small bottle of smelling salts from his pocket. He waved the vile stuff under my nose; I coughed and snapped out of my semi-stupor.

"Enough- please!" I requested. "I think I'm going to be sick."

"Do you want to go to the bathroom?"

"No, I need water," I said.

At that moment uniformed policemen, paramedics and a raft of other official people came storming into my department. Only four minutes had passed since my call. They must have been parked outside. Some librarians and a few patrons that had wandered in after the doors opened at nine tried to get in, but they were all turned away. Police were stationed at the doors. I sat in a room with about 20 men and a dead body. Did someone have a vendetta against librarians? Were we all going to be killed off, one by one, day by day?

Hugo and Scarlett appeared at my side.

"What's happened?" Scarlett said.

"Violetta, are you all right?" Hugo was shouting.

McGuire walked up with a cup of water.

"How the hell did they get in here?" he demanded.

"There's a secret door in my office," I said. He handed me the paper cup. "Stay put," he said to them sternly and stormed away.

"What happened?" Scarlett repeated.

I put my face in my hands. "It's Mark de Winter," I said. "He's dead."

"WHAT?" they both shrieked.

"He's dead, it's horrible. He's been run through with a sword."

They both stared at me in horror.

"You're kidding," Hugo said at last. "He's been stabbed?"

"I'm not kidding," I said, spitting into a tissue. "He's been stabbed in the throat with a fencing sword."

McGuire returned. His face was a mask of stone.

"You're going to have to stay here for a while. This is a crime scene and no one goes in or out without my permission. Please stay off the phone." He looked at me and for the first time today looked a bit human. "Feeling better?"

"Yes, thank you," I said. But my stomach was in knots and I kept trying to spit something that tasted awful out of mouth. I picked up another tissue and held it against my lips.

"I'll get an officer to take you to the bathroom in a minute," he said. "You look like you're going to be sick."

With those words, I picked up the small wastebasket under the desk, put my head into it and threw up my tea, toast and the oatmeal I had eaten at home this morning.

Chapter Eleven

A library is but the soul's burial-ground. It is the land of shadows.

-Henry Ward Beecher

Today was the longest day of my life. We sat in the Reference and Reading Room waiting. This time there were no intervening calls from the University President or the Mayor. The library was closed until further notice. The few patrons who had entered had all been questioned and had been asked to wait in the cafeteria with uniformed police officers. Most had complied; a few dissenters had given their vital information and had left.

Mrs. Vandermeer had appeared at the door of my department but she was not allowed to enter. The doors were shut and that was it. No one was able to come in without McGuire's approval. Or leave, either. I sat with Scarlett and Hugo and tried to feel something, but I was beyond panic or fear. I was numb. An officer brought me a cup of tea, ginger ale and a plate of crackers. I thanked him. I was sure McGuire had been responsible for this. A paramedic offered me oxygen and tried to take my blood pressure, but I waved him away. I just wanted to sit with my head buried in my hands and not do anything. The garbage can had been taken away but not before I saw the contents being emptied into an official looking zip-lock bag.

Didn't I own the rights to my own vomit?

"What are they doing?" I asked.

"They probably want to make sure you haven't been poisoned," Scarlett said. My eyes widened in shock and I picked up another tissue.

Hugo was cheerfully reading a library copy of *The Hound of the Baskervilles* and eating all my crackers.

"I'm sure no one poisoned Violetta," he said. "Arsenic gives you the runs."

"Thank you for sharing that with us, Hugo," I said. I wanted to stuff him into the book drop under the desk. "Quit eating all my crackers." I grabbed the plate and nibbled the corner off a saltine.

A few hours passed. I was feeling better but still woozy. McGuire was very busy and paid little attention to us. I had to go to the bathroom so I raised my hand and snagged an officer and made my request. Within minutes, a female officer came and offered to escort me to the ladies room.

"Can I come, too?" Scarlett asked. She could and she did. To add insult to injury another officer came and sat with Hugo while we were gone. I'm sure they thought he'd start tampering with the old card catalog or start deleting the files of our overdue patrons.

Inside the staff bathroom I went into the stall and sat for a while. I was practically dozing when a knock at the door brought me back to reality.

"Miss, are you all right?"

"I'm fine, I'm just so tired I can't even go," I said.

"It's shock," said the officer. "It dries you up."

"Thanks for telling me." I sat for a while and finally got the deed done. I came out and went to the sink and splashed cold water on my face. Scarlett wet a paper towel and held it against the back of my neck. The officer asked me again if I needed a doctor. I told her I just wanted to go home. Actually I wanted to talk to my mother and I wanted to go home and brush my teeth.

"I'm sure you can all leave in a little while," she said. I didn't believe her.

We trod back to the department and I was escorted back to my seat at the circulation counter. Hugo wasn't there. I peered over the edge of the counter and could just about see Hugo having a chat with McGuire in my office. The nerve, setting up an interview room in my private space. And without asking. He would hear about this, when I felt like myself again.

After a while, Hugo returned looking chastened. "Boy, is that guy tough!" he said. "No sense of humor, at all."

"Hugo, this is a murder investigation, not a tea party," I said.

"That's what he said," he scoffed and went back to eating a plate of those horrible little peanut butter and cheese crackers that they sell in vending machines. He was also guzzling Dr. Pepper, something he swore he never drank. Our lavish lunch compliments of the Chicago Police Department and the Midwestern University Library. No pizza brought up here today.

Another officer appeared. He stepped near us and his head became stained with the sapphire light from an overhead Tiffany window. We all blinked. He looked like an angel or a vampire depending on where you were sitting. *Geez, how many of them were skulking around the library?*

"Miss Prendergast, ma'am?" he was speaking to me. I pointed a finger in Scarlett's direction. "Miss Prendergast?" he repeated.

"Yes?" she said. Even Scarlett was beginning to look tired.

"Detective McGuire will see you now," he said.

"Will he, now?" she asked with a fine imitation of an Irish brogue.

The cop looked startled and then laughed.

"Keep it up, girl," I admonished. "We'll be in Joliet tonight."

"Oh, no," she cooed. "I want to go to that VIP prison where Martha Stewart went."

"Fat chance," I said.

Scarlett was gone and Hugo was too busy reading the *Hound* and enjoying himself to do me any good. Five, ten minutes passed by. I decided I would try and work on my book order. I wanted to browse some publisher's catalogs in my office. I stood up and gingerly made my way to the back. I looked quickly down the aisle behind the book stacks but it appeared the sliced and diced remains of Mark de Winter had been removed. I let out a breath.

"Excuse me," I said sweetly at the door of my office.

"Yes? Do you need something?" McGuire asked. Scarlett was sitting looking subdued. He had probably been giving her hell. Politely.

"Yes," I said and then I was yelling. Dammit, my Greek temper had been roused. "Yes! I would like to go home or get to work or do something than just sit here and rot all day! I mean, I know there was a murder, a terrible, terrible murder," I touched the tissue again to my lips, "but I can't sit here all day like a prisoner! I can't breathe, I'm getting anxious, I'm getting mad, and how long do we have to sit here? And who told you, that you could use my office and sit at my desk?" I was in a tizzy, I was doing fine. I could sing *Lady Macbeth* or *Tosca,* I was that stoked with anger.

"I'm sorry," he said, "I should have asked you first. But you were feeling sick and I needed someplace private, and I thought you wouldn't mind," he smiled engagingly. I still wanted to smash him. The whole library smelled of rubbing alcohol and some other weird scent.

"What is that odor?"

He sniffed. "Probably the powder and spray used for fingerprints."

"It's horrible and probably carcinogenic."

"I'm sure it isn't," he said softly. "You know, Miss Prendergast," he said. "I think Miss Aristotle looks tired. I'm going to question her now and then send her home. Would you mind if we finished talking a little later?"

"Absolutely not," Scarlett said. "I think that's a great idea."

"I would like to send you and Mr. Haydn home in a little while," he said. "We're almost finished here."

Scarlett left the office and I sank down into the seat she vacated. I never sit at this end of the desk and I looked at the pictures of my mom and dad and Siegfried on the wall and the pictures of Samson and Delilah on my desk. I had an Elvis pencil holder and mouse pad. A pink ballerina lamp from the 50's complete with tutu and a turquoise lava lamp sat on the credenza behind my desk. A large purple Chinese Deco rug with orange and green flowers and a pagoda with flying cranes ran the length of my small office. It was vintage and it was me.

"I like your office," he said, watching me.

"Did you dust it for prints?" I said, with an attitude. I was acting shabby but I couldn't stop myself.

"I don't think we need do that, right now," he said. He picked up his BlackBerry. "I'll make this brief, Violetta, and then I'm sending you home."

"Great," I said. I felt like crying.

"You arrived here this morning at 8:00, you went to the cafeteria first for a cup of tea, and then you went to the auditorium and did not come to the Reference and Reading Room until approx. 8:51. Is that correct?"

"Sounds good to me," I said.

"What happened when you got here?"

I had to cooperate. I had to. This was important. I can't lose it.

She looks so beat up. I'd like to take her home myself and tuck her into bed. Two dead bodies in two days? And both her colleagues? Poor baby.

I sensed his sympathy and it broke me up. I took out a wad of tissues and began to cry. "I don't know what's the matter with me, I never cry like this."

"You have a good reason to," he said softly. "Do you think you feel well enough to keep going on?"

I took a deep breath. "Yes," I said. "I walked in the library and I went to put my coat and bag in my office." I saw they were both sitting on a chair where I had left them. "I had a bag with today's newspapers and I wanted to go put them out in the Reading Room. But then I thought I'd get a book cart to clear out some of the old papers and magazines. I wanted to do something," I told him, "I wanted to move around. I didn't want to sit at my desk and think."

"That's understandable," he said, typing away.

"The book carts are housed at the back of the stacks, out of the way," I said. "We keep about 10 because this is a big department. So I decided to go get one and when I walked to the end of the stacks-" here I wiped away a tear, "there he was, lying there. He was stretched out on the cart, with the sword sticking out of his throat. The sword in the stone," I said, irrationally. "Excalibur."

"Did you touch the body?"

"NO! I just looked at him and then got away, as fast as I could, but I couldn't move my legs very well and got to the desk and called 911. I knew you were in the building but I couldn't trust myself to get to the hallway, I was afraid that I was going to pass out. And then I sat and waited. You came very quickly."

"We didn't have that far to go," he said. "Thank you, Violetta; I want you to go home now."

"Right now?"

"I'm going to get an officer to drive you and Miss Prendergast home," he said.

"We live in opposite directions," I said. "She's in Bridgeport and I'm in Lakeview."

"That's all right," he said. "She won't mind, and I don't want you to go home alone."

"I'm not a weakling," I said. "I used to go mountain climbing." *Great, Violetta, like he cares?*

With that dead husband of hers, I suppose, bird watching. Such a beautiful woman, couldn't he have taken her to Paris instead?

"I know you're strong but you've had two shocks in two days. I want you to go home and rest. Go home and see your parents and eat a little soup. And stay home tomorrow."

I looked at him in surprise. "Is that a suggestion or an order?"

"I'm going to request that your department be closed for a couple of days. I'm going to go talk to the director now. Wait here and I'll arrange your ride."

"We can't be closed!" I protested. "It's almost time for semester exams!"

"Try not to worry about the students," he said and left me. He obviously didn't know my devotion to my students. The department would have to remain open.

After 10 minutes I was summoned by another uniformed police officer.

"Ma'am?" he asked politely.

"Yes?"

"I'm here to take you home," he said.

I got my cape and book bags and tried to make a graceful exit. Scarlett was sitting by the desk. Hugo was gone.

"Where's Hugo?"

"He was sent home about five minutes ago."

I looked at the clock, it was almost three.

"I wonder if Mrs. Vandermeer is going to pay us?"

"She'll have to do something or the union will blast her. It's not our fault the library is closed," Scarlett said.

"Perhaps, but I'd hate to see a reduced paycheck. I've got a mortgage to pay and the taxes keep rising."

"I know," she agreed. "Maybe we can make up the time one night, if she decides to dock us."

I felt myself getting upset again. It wasn't our fault that Wilde and now de Winter were found dead in the Reference and Reading Room was it? It was fate, cruel fate, that had sent a murderer on a rampage in my department. McGuire, well, it was too early to tell if he was sent by cruel fate or beautiful destiny.

As if the day wasn't bad enough, Mrs. Vandermeer was standing by the swipe-in machine.

"Miss Aristotle and Miss Prendergast," she said, always formal. "Since the Reference and Reading Room is closed tomorrow I would like you to report to World Language. You can help them with their re-cataloging project."

Scarlett nodded and I stared at the southern belle in shock. Work in another department, cataloging? After the horrors we went through today? *I would rot in hell first.* I opened my mouth to speak but Scarlett was dragging me out the door.

A cute policeman name Malone drove us home in an unmarked car. We cruised up Lake Shore Drive. The sun was gleaming on the turquoise water and its brilliance blinded my tear-soaked eyes. Scarlett kept up a pleasant conversation with the man but I could only stare out the window and blow my nose.

"Cubs fans?" he asked us.

"Violetta is a Cubs fans, but I live on the south side so naturally I'm a Sox fan," she told him.

"I live south, too," he said. "Been a Sox fan all my life."

Hurray, I wanted to shout. I used to go ballgames with Siegfried but that's another thing I haven't done since his untimely demise. I seemed to be attracting death like hollyhocks attracted hummingbirds.

They talked about pizza and my dad's restaurant and if the new mayor was doing a good job. They were very chummy and I realized that he was maybe only 7 or 8 years younger than Scarlett and that she was enjoying herself immensely.

We got to my house in less than 15 minutes. When there's no traffic I live very close to downtown. Officer Malone pulled up in front of my house. I got my stuff.

"I'll walk you inside, ma'am," he said.

"There's no need, I'm fine," I said, but he got out of the car anyway. Scarlett started to get out, too, but he waved her back inside.

"It's all right, ma'am," he said to her. "I can do this."

"Call me Scarlett," she said demurely. He gave her a smile that said "I'm interested." She tucked a strand of hair behind her ear and lowered her gaze. I was ready to offer them a bedroom. How could she forget Beethoven so quickly?

I followed him impassively to the door. I took out my keys and heard my babies start to bark. He stood aside politely as I went through the hall door and grabbed their collars so they wouldn't jump all over him. He went into every room on the first floor. While I petted the pups and they greeted me in total delirium he went upstairs. Without a word and without permission, who did these guys think they were?

"Are you looking for something?" I was peeved.

"No ma'am, I am just following orders. Detective McGuire told me to check out your house and your friend's, too."

"What are you looking for?"

"Well- we just want to make sure the premises are secure."

Two people have been murdered, dummy, how do you know you're not next?

"Do you have a basement?"

I pointed to the door in the hallway. He ran down and returned quickly.

"Everything's locked," he said. "Do you need anything else?"

Just peace and quiet.

"I'm fine," I said. "Thank you."

Chicago's finest left the building and I did, too.

I got the leashes and took Samson and Delilah out for a walk. Naturally, we ended up at my mother's house. Naturally when she opened the door and I saw her concerned, beautiful face I burst into tears.

Chapter Twelve

"I am half sick of shadows," said the Lady of Shalott.

-Tennyson

I awoke to the delicious smell of coffee, second time today. I first smelt coffee at 4:30 a.m. before my father left for the restaurant. My mother always gets up to have breakfast with him and then goes back to sleep. I had slept in my old room in my old bed with the dogs curled around my feet. I had slept like a stone and had only awakened when my mom let the dogs out at 7 and when I had called in sick at 7:30. I could not face working in another department doing tedious cataloging under the direction of the Witches of Endor, as I liked to refer to the three women who ran the World Language Department. I never knew the difference between a French accent *aigu è* or an accent *grave é.* And I didn't care. I'm rotten at filing, too.

It was nine. I hadn't slept this late in years. My pooches were probably with my mother waiting for her to drop something on the kitchen floor. I got out of bed and put on my yellow plush Winnie-the-Pooh slippers. My black nightgown just about covered my tush. I liked to have room to swing my long legs while I slept. I walked into the kitchen. Mick McGuire, my mom and Samson and Delilah were sitting and having a cozy cup of coffee and a few pounds of Greek toast. I tried to sneak out but it was too late, my dogs had seen me. They jumped up ecstatically to greet me like I was Snow White awakening from a long sleep. I pulled at my shirt because I saw McGuire was checking out my legs.

"I'll get you a robe," my mother said, while I stood there frozen to the kitchen floor.

"Good morning," he said and poured me a cup of coffee.

Cozy again. We were getting positively domestic, the Aristotle and McGuire clans.

"Good morning," I said cautiously. I looked out the window, the day was grey and the skies overcast. "What's so good about it? It looks like hell outside."

"Cream? Sugar?" he put the cup down next to him on the table.

I slid into the chair quickly and picked up the cream. After getting the coffee the right medium beige color I picked it up and took a cautious sip. "Thank you," I mumbled into my cup.

"Toast?" he put two thick slices of the sesame seed covered Greek bread on a plate and put it in front of me. He seemed very comfortable waiting on me and I wondered if he had made his ex-wife breakfast in bed. I shivered.

"Cold?"

"No," I said, tugging at my nightgown.

He smiled and threw two dog biscuits to Samson and Delilah.

"They're on a diet," I said.

He winked at me and I wanted to shake him.

My mother returned with my father's plaid robe. "Here, honey," she said. "It's kind of chilly this morning."

And my butt is showing. As my father would say, *keep them guessing*, but there was little to guess about the length and size of my long, healthy legs. McGuire had seen every inch of them by now.

"Thanks, Mom," I said and bit into the hot, buttery toast.

"I called you last night but you weren't home," Mick said. "So then I tried your parents' house. Your mother told me you were resting, and I didn't want to bother you. I told your mother," here he smiled at Sophia and she beamed back at him, "that I would come see you today."

"And here you are," I said, still in a very bad mood. "More news?"

"I'm afraid I do have something to tell you," he said cautiously. "Your friend Miss Prendergast was brought in for questioning last night. Only her prints and Wilde's were found on his walking stick."

"What does that mean?" I said, choking on hot coffee. I coughed for a while and he affably patted my back. I wanted him to stop but I couldn't talk so I sat there like a big fool until the spasm subsided. Finally I could speak. "You know she picked up the stick when we moved the body."

My mother's eyes widened like spotlights at the Lyric, but she didn't ask. Not yet, anyway. I would be grilled later.

"Yes, but we would expect to find other prints, those of his wife or his colleagues in History," said McGuire. Everyone said that he often left the walking stick all over the History Library and that it was always being returned to him."

"Is that so?" I said, chomping on more toast. My dogs sat at my feet waiting for crumbs to drop. "So maybe Wilde had polished the walking stick before the party and only Scarlett and his prints remained."

"That's possible, but I think the stick was polished after he was dead. And I think your friend Miss Prendergast knows more about that than you know."

"What are you getting at?"

"You're not going to like this, Violetta," he said. "But last night your friend admitted to hitting Wilde over the head with his walking stick after the party Monday night."

"WHAT?" I put my cup down with shaking hands. "She admitted to what?"

"She admitted that she and Wilde," he pulled out his BlackBerry, "had an altercation around 9:45pm. He became abusive, tried to "molest" her as she put it, and in self-defense she picked up his walking stick where it lay against a chair and struck him with it. Then she ran out of your department. She swears he was standing when she left him, rubbing his head, yelling curses at her."

"I don't believe it," I said. "Why didn't she tell me?"

"Because when you two found him dead two days ago she was afraid that the blow he had received when she struck him had killed him."

My mother picked up the coffee pot and refilled our cups. She was unnaturally silent, a sure sign that she was shocked. I was unusually silent myself, a sure sign that I was in a state of total disbelief and bewilderment.

"So she admitted to hitting him," I said at last.

"That's right," he said.

"And she thought she had killed him."

"Yes. That's the idea."

"And after we moved the body and she moved the walking stick she decided to wipe the stick clean because…"

"Why do you think?"

"Because she thought she had killed him and she didn't want her prints to be found on what she thought was a murder weapon," I said. My brain was starting to work again.

"Exactly," he smiled encouragingly.

"Will she be charged with something?" My heart was pounding.

"We're not sure yet," he said cautiously.

"Is she in jail?"

"No, she's home, or maybe with Peter Lancaster. He came with her last night and took her to his home afterwards." I wanted to call her desperately. I looked at the phone longingly.

McGuire smiled. "I'm leaving soon; you can call your friend and check on her."

"I can't believe Scarlett struck Wilde with his walking stick. Where was everybody else? Where was Dolly?" I asked.

"Mrs. Wilde, ahem," he coughed, "went home alone. She thought that Mr. Wilde would be staying the night with Roxanne de Winter. He often did that," he explained to the two women.

"The snake," I said. "He didn't even sleep at home."

"Not all the time, but a couple of times a week," Mick said.

"What a man!" my mother said.

"You can say that again," I said.

"He could be amusing," Sophia said. "He knew a lot about the opera and actually had seen me sing many years ago. I think he knew how to flatter women."

"If you say so," I said. "Why was he trying to attack Scarlett the night of the party?"

"He had a blood alcohol concentration of 0.9," McGuire said. "He was legally intoxicated," he told us neophytes. "Wilde followed Ms. Prendergast into the Reference and Reading Room and tried to rekindle an old flame. She was a challenge to him because she was in love with Peter Lancaster. Wilde wanted to take her away from him so he could have total control over Lancaster's life, I guess. At least that's what Ms. Prendergast says," he amended.

"Wilde was drunk?" my mother asked.

"Yes, legally so," he said.

"Maybe that's why he wanted to get close to Scarlett, she is a lovely woman." My mother was trying to be helpful.

"Champagne sped up the effects of the arsenic," he told us. "Wilde died not long after the blow to the head."

"Scarlett never would hurt a fly," I said.

"She's a weight lifter," he said. "She's very strong."

"Meaning what?" I said.

"Meaning her tap on the head as she called it was enough to cause a head trauma and a concussion. Wilde probably passed out from the blow and then suffocated on his vomit from the arsenic."

I buried my face in my hands. "I don't want to talk about it anymore." I was getting a queasy feeling in my stomach. "You know what, Mom; I think I'm going to go home."

"Stay, Violetta, I don't have any students until this afternoon. You can rest and I'll make you soup."

I stood up and pushed my arms into the robe. "Thanks, Ma, but I want to go home and die in my own bed."

Sophia gasped and McGuire grabbed my arm.

"Only a figure of speech," I assured them. "I just mean I'm tired and I'm going to sleep away the day with my dogs."

"Don't scare us," my mother admonished.

"I'll walk you home," he said

"You don't have to," I said. "I'll be fine."

"I insist," he said in a voice that brooked no interference.

"Let Mick walk you home, Violetta," my mother implored. "The streets are so quiet this time of morning," she shuddered delicately. I knew she expected that I would encounter any number of wandering footpads and assassins on the way home. I sighed and stomped out of the room. When I returned dressed in yesterday's clothes he was waiting. Mom and he looked very chummy. She probably had heard all about his divorce and who he had dated since then. Sophia is very good at getting people to talk about themselves and they don't even realize they've been spilling their guts out to her.

"Ready, dear?" she asked. She had put Samson and Delilah on their leashes for me and they sat waiting, tongues hanging out in anticipation of their walk. I picked up my cape and threw it around my shoulders before McGuire could try his cavalier act again. I didn't want to get too close to him this morning.

I kissed her goodbye. "Thanks, Mom. I'll call you soon."

"Come over later," she said. "I'm making meat loaf." She smiled at Mick. "You're welcome, too," she said.

"Thanks, Mrs. Aristotle," he said. "I'll probably be working but I appreciate your offer."

"I'll save you some," she said happily.

I gave her the eye as I followed him out the front door. She giggled.

"Let's take the car," he said. "I've got to get back downtown in a little while."

"I can walk," I said. "No problem."

"Don't start, Violetta," he said. "Get in, please." He opened the back door for the dogs. I didn't want to start an argument with him when I was sure my mother was hanging out behind the lace curtains watching us. I didn't want to start an argument because I still felt like crying and I did not want to disgrace myself again in front of him. He would think I was just a weakling and I had too much pride for that. Not that I had been emotion free the past two days since we met. Since Tuesday morning I had cried, laughed, puked, lied, been rude and had screamed at him like a banshee. *No wonder he was keeping his distance, he probably thought I was psycho.*

I hate to leave her alone, she looks so lost. I wish I could stay with her.

I got into the back seat with the dogs and buried my nose in their curly fur.

"Ready?" he sat and drove the few blocks to my house in silence.

When we pulled up he said, "I'd like to talk to you for a minute, Violetta."

"OK." I said. "What do you want to talk about?"

"I'll walk you inside," he said.

"Do you really think someone is waiting inside the door ready to hit me over the head, poison me or run me through with a sword?"

"I don't know," he said. "That's why I want to walk you inside."

I felt helpless but I complied with his wishes. The dogs bounded through the door and I waited while he checked the upstairs and downstairs of my house. He went through the basement while I went and brushed my teeth. When I came out of the bathroom he was waiting, quickly browsing the morning paper.

"Speed reader?" I said. My repartee stunk this morning.

He smiled. "Not really, don't have much time to read when I'm on an investigation, so I have to skim for information."

"I see," I said and folded my arms across my chest. I longed to get out of this ruffled skirt. "So what do you think is going to happen to me and my colleagues?"

"I'm not sure," he said. "That's why I want you to be very careful. I can understand Wilde having enemies, but outside of Wilde, de Winter really didn't seem to have any. That's what's so puzzling." He seemed to be talking half to me and half to himself. "Unless-"

"Unless what?"

"Unless Mark de Winter discovered something about Wilde's death and the murderer decided to silence de Winter."

"Whose sword was it that killed Mark?"

"We're still trying to trace it. It didn't belong to Wilde or de Winter. It appeared to be made out of the country, maybe from South America."

"The case of the mysterious rapier, it sounds like an old thriller," I groaned.

"Read many of those?" he asked, a small smile softening his stern face.

"Agatha Christie and Dorothy L. Sayers are two of my favorites," I admitted. "And of course you can't beat Sir Arthur Conan Doyle."

"Yes, I always wanted to live like Lord Peter Wimsey," he agreed. "Live in a fancy house, have a man servant, drive a Rolls, it would be sweet. Instead, I'm more on a Watson-esque budget.

"You're a very cultured man," I said.

"For a policeman, right?" Now he looked amused.

"No, just in general," I said.

"You wouldn't say that to one of your librarian friends."

"Librarians are supposed to be wimpy and read a lot of old books and listen to the opera," I retorted. "We're not quarterbacks or police detectives by nature."

"And yet you went mountain climbing to see wild, rare birds," he said, pointing to a picture on the wall of me and Siegfried, on top of a hill in Costa Rica. "That was adventurous and possibly dangerous at times."

"That was Siegfried," I said. "He motivated me to take chances and see the world."

"And now?"

"I kind of lost my taste for travel after he died. I've been to Memphis once to see Elvis and once to Florida to see my cousins. I've become a homebody."

"That's OK," he said softly, "you have a nice home. I'd like to come back one evening after this is over and listen to you play the piano."

"Who told you I played?" *As if I didn't know. The Italian canary had probably filled him in on everything but my bra size.*

"Your mother mentioned it," he said.

"I play a little," I said.

He walked up close and picked up a strand of hair off my shoulders. "I'd like to take you to dinner one night, somewhere quiet with candles and a nice bottle of wine."

I took a deep breath. His lime scent was intoxicating and I felt so woozy. I started to sway a little. He reached out and put his hands on my shoulders.

"Steady, there, are you sure you're all right?"

I was until you touched me.

I could hold her all day and night, she feels so good.

"I'm fine. I guess I'm still a bit tired after yesterday."

"Shock is a terrible thing," he said. "And you had a big one."

"I should be tougher, I must!" I said, but I felt tears prick the back of my eyes.

"You're tough enough, believe me," he said. "I wouldn't want you any tougher."

"Why not?"

"I like feminine, spunky women."

Is that so? So why not do something about it?

"I see," I said. He dropped his hands.

"What are you going to do now?" he asked me.

"I'm going to take a hot shower and I hope finally to get to work on that book order!"

"OK, Miss librarian, but be careful. Don't open the door to any strangers or to anyone from the library."

"You don't think any of them would try to murder me?"

"I don't know, but I don't want to take that chance. Nobody in your house except the family."

"How about Scarlett?"

"I think she's probably going to be busy today."

"More questions?"

"Yes, we need to question her again."

"Didn't you talk to her long enough last night?" I was getting upset and it showed.

He put his large, warm hands on my shoulders again. "Now, Violetta, sweetheart, please don't be mad. But you have to realize, your friend struck a man. It would have been manslaughter but he had already been poisoned. Now I have to wait to see if the district attorney wants to press any charges. I can't do any more or less right now."

Had he called me sweetheart? Wow.

"Just be nice to her," I said, "she's really a wonderful person and takes care of her old parents. She visits them every day." *Get out the violins.*

"I'm sure she's a great woman and a great friend," he said soothingly. He had pulled me close and was rubbing my shoulder blades. My dogs sat on the dining room rug and watched us. I felt myself melting into his hands. I leaned closer and lay my chin on his strong shoulder. I sighed.

"Feeling better?" he whispered in my ear.

Yes and no. I was feeling desire, the first time in five years and frankly, I was feeling very anxious. *Was there any Paxil in the house?*

Chapter Thirteen

Opaa!

-Greek saying of happiness

I was tired after Mick left me. I took a hot shower and sat down in front my computer. There were numerous emails from Scarlett, sent from the library and from Peter's house. They were rambling about how she was sorry she hadn't told me about the incident with Wilde but she didn't want to get me in trouble.

Oh really? Like I wasn't in enough trouble already.

I sent her a very bland email back in case these were all being read by unknown police cyber hackers downtown. I told her not to worry and that I would talk to her soon. I thought about her smacking Wilde over the head and wondered exactly what he had said to move her to violence. She really isn't that kind of person at all.

The sun broke through the clouds and my little office became suffused with sunlight. My dogs slept peacefully at my feet and I became enthused about books and started working on a book order. I loved ordering books on-line, it's like the entire world of knowledge and information is at my fingertips. I worked for hours and just when I was starting to need a break the doorbell rang.

Who could it be at this hour? It was just noon and everyone I knew was either at work or in police custody. I sighed and went to the front hall. The dogs were barking in anticipation. I shoved them behind the hall door and went to check. Through the glass window on the door I could see the spiky head of Hugo.

Without hesitation, I opened the door.

"Hugo, hi, why aren't you at work? Are you sick?"

"Violetta, I took half a day off, I told them I wasn't feeling well. But really I wanted to see if you were O.K. I called you last night but you weren't home."

He stood on the doorstep smiling. In his hands were two shopping bags.

"I stayed at my parents' last night," I told him. "What's in the bags?"

"Lunch," he said happily and without asking, walked into my house.

"Lunch?"

"You know, food to eat," he said and headed straight for the kitchen.

Samson and Delilah followed Hugo eagerly sniffing the bags. He put the food on the kitchen island and looked very happy.

"You didn't have to do that, Hugo," I said.

"I know, but I wanted to," he said, unpacking cartons from the bags. "Can I have two plates, please?"

I complied and took out some serving spoons.

"Smells good, what is it?"

"I stopped to see your Dad, before I came up here. I told him I wanted to bring you lunch and he insisted on packing the food himself."

"Really? That was nice of you, Hugo. Pop sent enough food to feed an army." I wanted to ask Hugo why he had gone to see my dad, but then that would have exposed his motivation to try and score a free lunch for us, so I kept quiet. There were numerous containers and cartons. Dad had sent enough food for six people.

"I know, isn't that great?" He kept unwrapping food and then pulled a bottle of ouzo out of the bag. He saw me looking at the bottle of anise flavored Greek liqueur and smiled. "Your Dad said this was good for shock."

"I'm not in shock, really, except for the fact you're here with food and drink for me."

"Why should that be shocking?" Hugo asked. "You know how fond I am about you, Violetta."

"What is it about me, lately?" I said half to myself.

"I know, you've got that big cop looking at you all the time. Really, I'm quite jealous." He giggled and screwed open the cap on the bottle of ouzo. He took two glasses from the wine glass rack and poured.

"Isn't it kind of early?"

"Naw, it's after 12 o'clock," he said. "A little aperitif before lunch will be good for you."

I took the glass of ouzo and added a little water to dilute the strong milky white liquid. I took a cautious sip. The strong anise flavor which I love, delivered an immediate punch. I started to cough.

"Easy now," Hugo said and patted me on the back.

"I'm fine," I gasped, and patted my chest. Hugo's eyes watched me appreciatively. I was glad I had on a loose sweatshirt for he took a great interest in my wardrobe and an even greater interest in what lay beneath my usual black garments.

"You need to sip it," he said and laughed again. He took a tiny drink from his glass. His eyes were shining. I wondered if he had already taken a drink today; he seemed so pleased with himself, even more than usual.

I took a plate and put some Greek salad and grilled chicken breast on it. I wasn't sure how hungry I was but I could always manage something. Hugo had piled his plate with salad, chicken, cheese, bread and *pastitio*, a nutmeg flavored Greek *lasagna.* We sat on stools that flanked the butcher block kitchen island.

For a thin man he could really pack it away and for a few minutes he ate in silence. I sipped ouzo and ate slowly. My dogs sat at our feet waiting for something to drop. It was odd but they never rushed up to Hugo like they did to my other friends. They kept their distance from him.

After popping an olive into his mouth and spitting the pit across the room into the garbage can like a kid, he smiled and sighed.

"Man, I love Greek food," he said. "Your dad's food is great."

"I'm glad you think so," I said, spearing a lettuce leaf with my fork. "Would you like some coffee or tea?"

"Tea, please," he said but he refilled our glasses with ouzo. I put the kettle on to boil. My, weren't we cozy, sitting in my kitchen, drinking, eating and hanging out with my dogs. It didn't seem possible that we had two murders in our library in two days.

"I can't believe what's happened," Hugo said, reading my thoughts. "Who do you think is the murderer?" His green eyes lit up with interest. "Do you think Peter finally snapped and did it?"

"I have no idea who *did it,"* I said with emphasis, trying not to relive the two incidents in my mind. "I don't- I prefer not to think that any of my colleagues or friends could do something so evil," I said. "I hope it was some stranger who wandered in-"

"And started picking off librarians?"

"Something like that," I said. Hugo shrugged and looked skeptical. "Now look," I said, "random acts of violence occur every day, you just have to read the newspapers. Why couldn't some person have hidden in the library and waited until after it closed and then-"

"Started bumping off random librarians? And why in our department?"

"Why, indeed," I said and started unraveling the braid that hung over my shoulder. "There has to be a connection between the two deaths."

"But what?" Hugo said. "Maybe Mark killed Wilde because he was eaten up with jealousy about Roxanne and snapped."

"But then who killed Mark?"

"How about Dolly?"

"No, I don't think that's possible," I said. "I can't see Dolly running someone through with a sword, for God's sake. She's too tender-hearted."

"Is she?" Hugo said, taking a swig of his hot tea, then a sip of ouzo. "People aren't always what they seem, Violetta. You're too trusting."

"Am I?" I said. "I thought I was as tough as nails."

He gave me an *are you kidding look* and I went into the bathroom. When I came back I was combing out the tangles in my hair. I sat down and continued my chore in silence. Hugo reached over and picked up a hank of my wavy hair that had tumbled past my shoulders to trail down the middle of my back.

"I hate to tell you this, Violetta, but you've got split ends."

"Do I? Does it matter?"

"Of course it matters; you've got such gorgeous hair you need to take care of it better. You need deep conditioning and a haircut."

I sighed. "I suppose you're right."

"How long has it been since you've been to a salon?"

"Not since my husband died, you know that."

"Yes, you did tell me once but I had forgotten how long ago that was. Isn't it time to rejoin the living?"

"Why, so I can become one of the dead?" I laughed, without humor. "You or I could be next, Hugo, and we don't even know why."

He looked at me and for once all the eager silliness in his eyes had been replaced with a shrewd intelligence. "Let's not talk about it anymore," he said. "I came here to cheer you up."

"You're right, you did," I said, trying a real smile.

"That's better," he said. He touched my hair again. "How about I give you a haircut?"

"What? You?"

"Why not? I can give you a trim. You need to cut off the split ends."

"I thought you had studied biology, not cosmetology."

"I'm very good with my hands. See? I do my own hair," he said pointing to his spiky do with pride. "I've been cutting my own hair for years. Come on, Violetta, let's do it, I'll just take off one teensy, tiny inch, I promise."

I looked at my hair. He was right. There were split ends. I needed a makeover.

"O.K.," I sighed. This was crazy. "What do we need?"

"Do you have some good scissors?"

"Actually, I do. I bought a pair to trim Samson and Delilah's hair."

He looked at me and the dogs like we were nuts.

"Of course you did," he said as if humoring a small, insane child. "Could you get them please?"

I went for the scissors and a couple of towels. When I came back into the kitchen, Hugo was thinking, I could tell, because the perpetual smile wasn't plastered on his face.

"You know, I think it would be better if you washed your hair first," he said. "Then I can be very sure to get the ends even."

I looked at the kitchen sink. "In there?"

"Sure, why not, would you like me to help you?"

"No, thank you, I can wash it myself." I thought of Hugo's nurturing hands in my hair and suppressed a laugh. I was truly losing it, allowing one of my junior librarians to give me a haircut. But I was game enough to stick my head under the faucet, wet it and pour a generous dollop of shampoo in my hands. The problem with very long hair is it takes forever to wash it and so I was busy scrubbing and rubbing and trying to rinse the soap out of the ends and couldn't hear anything except for the running water and Hugo singing a song from Sweeney Todd at the top of his lungs because he was so fond of Sondheim.

"Where did you put the scissors?' he yelled.

"On the table," I yelled back.

I put a towel over my head for a second to catch some of the water that was dripping down my face. I blotted and rubbed and gave Hugo another look. He was holding the scissors in his hand with a weird look on his face. I felt like I was having a déjà vu, but couldn't place it. I reached for the bottle of conditioner but all of a sudden there was a loud crashing at the back door. I screamed and whirled around. My black hair spewed streams of water around the kitchen like an outdoor sprinkler.

Hugo was standing rooted to the floor with the open scissors in his hand, water dripping off his glasses. The back door was now hanging half off its hinges, and the force of the wood as it exploded out of its frame filled the air with plaster and wood dust. I coughed and sneezed and brushed wood chips out of my wet eyes.

Standing there in the midst of it all was Mick McGuire, gun drawn and ready for action.

Chapter Fourteen

The reason so many people turned up at his funeral is that they wanted to make sure he was dead.

-Samuel Goldwyn

It was Friday night and I was at Hieronymus Wilde's memorial service at the Drake Hotel. It's a really fancy place for a funeral but then the hotel was a favorite of Wilde's. He liked to stuff himself on Lobster Newburg in the Cape Cod room and he had been known to buy his groupies many martinis while listening to Buddy Charles, the great piano player in the Coq d'Or. The place was packed with librarians, academics, a few politicians and family. I didn't know that Wilde had so many friends besides his women and his groupies.

We were in a tastefully appointed meeting room with French provincial chairs and sofas, Aubusson rugs and elegant candelabras on the walls. At the front of the room was a large table covered in a white velvet cloth. Sitting atop the velvet was a very large silver urn with intaglio handles. I had never seen a cremation urn and I was surprised at the size of it. I guess Wilde had made a lot of ashes.

At another table artfully displayed were many photographs in silver and black frames. There were some of Dolly and Wilde at their wedding but the majority was of Wilde, a retrospective of his "amazing life," as Dolly put it. I looked at him as a young man; masses of red-hair, perpetually smiling and I could see where he might have been thought romantically handsome. There was Wilde on safari in Kenya, Wilde at the Pyramids at Giza, Wilde standing proudly in front of the first computer in the History Department. There were many pictures of Wilde with his groupies and a small photograph of Wilde, Roxanne and Dolly holding champagne flutes.

I had made it into work today because Sgt. O'Leary had called me late last night to tell me the Reference and Reading Room would be open. I thought it significant that Mick had not called and had left the duty to his assistant. Of course, Mick was so disgusted and furious that I had let Hugo in and so angry that he had broken my door down that he probably never wanted to speak to me again. O'Leary had been very professional except when he asked me if my back door had been fixed. I had told him about the Irish carpenters that had arrived within the hour and how the entire door had been reset, repaired and repainted before the 6 p.m. news. Mick had sort of apologized to me about breaking and entering and had sort of apologized to Hugo for thinking he was about to murder me with a pair of scissors- but not really. Mick managed to make us think that he thought it was all *our fault* and that we should be the ones apologizing. What really pissed me off was that Mick called my mom and dad and they showed up and sat with me until the repairs were done. Hugo had left on his own steam but I could tell he was really hurt about what Mick thought about him.

Early this morning I had received a call from Corny, Mrs. Vandermeer's assistant telling me the Reference and Reading Room was open and ready for action. I acted like I didn't know and thanked him for the information.

"Are you feeling better?" he had asked me. "Can you come into work, Mrs. V. wants to know?"

I had said I would try and last the day. It wasn't easy but I made it. Two uniformed policemen were in the department all day. One sat in the center of the room reading magazines and another stood in the stacks behind the circulation desk picking his teeth. I don't know if they were expecting another dead body to materialize between the encyclopedias and the atlases but if they did, they were disappointed.

There were some students who came in to gawk and giggle, and a few journalists who tried to ask me some questions, but I hid in my office until they left. I had nothing to say. Mrs. Vandermeer had made a statement to the press and so had Mick McGuire. I was not expected to make some brilliant revelation on the demise of two librarians in two days in my department. And most people didn't know about me and Scarlett rolling over Wilde's body. That was classified info, I guess.

I hated wakes and funerals, but I always did my duty and showed up. So here I was standing in line waiting to pay my respects to Dolly. I was dressed in an appropriate black dress which was no problem for me as most my clothes were black these days. My hair was arranged into a French twist.

I waited alone. I had come here after work by myself and I would go home alone. I had called Scarlett yesterday and today on her cell phone, her home phone and at Peter's house but she hadn't returned my calls. I guess it was her turn to call in sick, but I hadn't gotten any messages. *Was she arrested for the attempted murder of Wilde? What had happened to her?* Neither she nor Peter had showed up tonight and nobody had talked to them today. *Was he an accomplice?* Now I was starting to have doubts. Maybe he did poison Wilde, after all, and Scarlett hit him over the head to hide the fact. I shivered.

I stood behind the Rileys, a tall, gaunt custodian and his rotund wife, the cafeteria lady, as we called her. They always reminded me of Jack Spratt and his wife. Lean and stout, tall and short, laconic and garrulous. He never spoke and she wouldn't stop talking. She was embracing Dolly Wilde heartily and blabbing non-stop about her great loss. Mr. Riley stood there smiling lugubriously, like Herman Munster.

At last it was my turn. Dolly was standing there, teary eyed, looking quite chic in a black silk dress and pearls. Her hair had been "done" and it was arranged in a very high wind-swept style, unlike her usual plain schoolgirl bob. She wore make-up and her nails had been painted a rosy pink. I was sure her two sisters, who flanked her sides like beefy buttresses, had been the cause of this makeover. They were also southern belles but they flaunted it. Diamonds twinkled on wrinkled hands, make-up was piled on Joan Collins style and their hair-dos were bleached cotton candy confections that Marie Antoinette would have envied.

I held out my hands and Dolly grabbed me.

"I'm so sorry, Dolly," I murmured into her neck. The smell of hair spray was overpowering.

"I know you are, Violetta," she said on a sob. She leaned back and looked straight into my eyes. "Who would have thought we'd both be widows? How cruel fate is to deal us both this unkind blow. First your beloved Siegfried and now my dear Hieronymus." She sighed. "This is my sister Daphne and my sister Delores," she said in quite a different tone of voice. They drawled hello and I did likewise. I looked at Dolly closely. Was she just enjoying being the center of attention a shade too much? Was she throwing herself into this new role of the Merry Widow with excess enjoyment?

Leave her alone, Violetta, she was under Wilde's thumb for many years, now she can be free and have a good time.

"I hope you are going to take some time off, Dolly," I said. "So you can rest and forget."

"I will never forget dear Hieronymus," she said, "but I would like to forget the terrible, tragic way he died," she whispered with crystal tears flooding her big baby blue eyes.

"We are taking her on a cruise next week," the sister called Daphne told me.

"We are going to South America. We will travel around Cape Horn and go to a tango convention in Buenos Aries. Some fresh sea air will do her a world of good," Delores added.

I thought of tsunamis and hurricanes but held my tongue. I thought of Dolly and her sisters tango-ing in Buenos Aires with roses between their big, white collective teeth and became hysterical. *Don't laugh.* I thought of Sigfried lying in a hospital bed while I had held his hand and cried and became serious again. I couldn't go on a cruise after a funeral. I would rather stay home and grieve. In fact, that's exactly what I did do. I stayed home for two months in my pajamas listening to opera and hardly eating until my father had come over and told me to rejoin the living. It had been torture to get dressed and go back to work but he had been right.

"I hope you will have a good time together," I said. "You know, we will all miss you very much at the library, Dolly."

"Bless you child, I'm coming back to work," she said, sounding more southern by the minute. After a couple of weeks with the two big D's she could fill in for Mrs. Vandermeer.

I kept staring at the silver urn. Dolly saw me looking at it.

"Yes, that's dear Hieronymus," she sighed. "I think I am going to take Hieronymus' office and make it into a room of remembrance," she said. "I will take his favorite books and papers and put them on a table in front of his special massaging Lazy-Boy lift chair," she said quite seriously. And in the middle-" She nodded at the urn. "What do you think, Violetta?"

"You must be crazy," I muttered under my breath.

"What do you say?"

"Amazing, that's an amazing idea, Dolly," I gushed. "How Hieronymus will love looking down on earth, seeing his room kept as a shrine for him." *I think I was going to be sick again.*

"Yes, that's it, exactly," she said. "A shrine to his greatness."

"You are such a devoted wife, Dolly." *She had loved him, of that I'm certain.*

"Hieronymus inspired devotion," she sighed. "I'll never find another man like him"

A librarian coughed discretely behind me. I guess I had talked enough.

"No, you'll never find another like him, he was an original," I agreed.

"You are coming to the buffet after the service, Violetta? It's upstairs in the Cape Cod room, Hieronymus' favorite place to eat."

I couldn't think of a decent excuse so I just nodded and smiled. She hugged me again and I escaped into the room. Chairs were lined up in rows and in the back I saw a couple of priests hanging out. I knew Hieronymus wasn't religious but Dolly was always talking about her church.

I almost tripped over Hugo as I walked in a daze to a seat.

"Violetta, psst! Here, come sit with me!" he said in a stage whisper that could be heard out on Michigan Avenue.

I dropped into the seat and put my hands on my hot cheeks. I was trying to stay calm but I wasn't sure if I could do it. *No crying here, please.*

"Did you get a hold of Scarlett?"

"No, I never did," I said. "I hope she's not in jail."

"Wouldn't your friend tell you if she was?" Hugo nodded at McGuire who had just come in the room and sat just a little closer to me. I felt a jolt like a mule had kicked me right in the guts. I could still hear his voice, dripping with disdain and anger as he chewed me out for letting Hugo in the house and for me being so stupid as to turn my back on him and stick my head in a freaking sink with the water running!

"No, they don't tell you anything," I said with a touch of malice. "They only want to know everything."

"Where's Peter Lancaster?" Hugo was looking around the room, his spiky hair sending out signals like antennas.

"Did you expect him to come tonight?" I said. "Knowing how much he hated Wilde?"

"I think if I was a major suspect in a murder investigation I would come and show my face. I would act like I was innocent," Hugo said. I looked at him. When did he get so shrewd?

"He is innocent, isn't he?" I riposted.

Hugo raised his eyebrows. "*Que sera, sera*, my dear. Time will tell. I see Roxanne has come tonight. She looks positively ghastly," he said with enjoyment. She was sitting alone in the back near two men that looked like cops. "When is the service for Mark?"

"I don't know," I said. "His family lives in St. Louis, maybe he'll be sent there." I could still see Mark lying there with a sword through his jugular.

"You can ask your friend, McGuire, he'll probably know."

"I'm sure he does," I said.

I saw McGuire talking to the two men in the back. They had been here when I arrived. Now I knew they were cops and I'm sure they were watching us all. Maybe they were expecting another murder to take place any minute. A priest walked up to the front of the room. We all fell silent. He walked up to the podium and took the microphone in his hands.

"Good evening," he began. "I am Father Wilson. Ladies and gentlemen we have come to say goodbye to our dear friend, Hieronymus Wilde." Dolly bravely raised a handkerchief to her eyes. Several of the groupies began crying. Roxanne was looking at the urn with a rapt expression. I wondered if we rubbed it three times a genie would appear.

"Hieronymus was a man who touched everyone he met," he continued.

"Literally," I muttered. Hugo snickered. I saw McGuire's eyes upon me. *Why couldn't we behave?*

"Hieronymus was a man of culture, of history and

of education. He was fond of quoting Oscar Wilde and Shakespeare. As a youth in college he played Romeo, Hamlet and several parts in Macbeth and Midsummer Night's Dream."

"He played the ass," Hugo whispered.

I shushed him and he giggled. This time the Rileys turned around and looked at us. I pulled my crystal rosary from my pocket and began rubbing the beads devoutly. If only Sister Millicent, my eighth grade teacher, could see me now she'd hit me with a ruler.

"We are not here to lament the passing of Hieronymus but to celebrate his new life," the priest went on in a fervent voice.

"I thought Catholics were against cremation," Hugo said.

"Dolly is Episcopalian," I said quietly.

"Hieronymus will be missed by his wife of 19 years, Dolly, by her sisters Daphne and Delores, by his numerous friends and colleagues and most of all by the patrons of the History Department of Midwestern University Library."

"Pause for applause," Hugo muttered. I felt like shouting hurray or olé or what the hey! but I kept my mouth shut. The sooner Father Wilson stopped talking the better. I did not want to disrespect the dead but I felt it extremely hypocritical to be sitting here acting mournful when all we really wanted to know was who put the arsenic in Pop's *kourabiedes*?

"*Who put the overalls in Mrs. Murphy's chowder*," I sang quietly.

"What are you singing?" Hugo nudged me. "*Tosca?*"

I opened my mouth to start another verse but then we were all being asked to stand and say the Lord's Prayer. I bent my head and tried to feel something. I felt a void where my love for Siegfried used to be and I felt revulsion for the way Wilde and de Winter had met their ends.

Here I was praying for a man who was both loved and hated and among our midst was a murderer. I prayed for salvation, enlightenment and maybe just one wild night with Mick McGuire before I joined the old maid's society and got a couple of cats to play with my dogs. The prayer ended and I felt a heavy hand on my shoulder. *An answer so soon to my prayers?*

It was Mick. He leaned over us. He had a long way to come down to meet my ear.

"Are you going to the buffet?" he asked.

"I don't think so," I said.

"Of course we are," Hugo said, putting his hand on my arm proprietorially. "I'm famished."

Between the two of them I could neither run nor hide.

Mick frowned at the hand on my arm.

"Of course we are," I heaved a sigh. "We're famished."

"I'll walk with you," Mick said. I stood up, and smoothed down my skirt.

"You don't have to," I said stiffly.

"But I want to," he said. I met his eyes briefly and felt that jolt of electricity again. Wasn't I mad at him?

"That's a nice dress, it fits you perfectly."

"It's supposed to be my Emma Peel dress," I said, blabbing away as usual.

"I should dress like John Steed with a bowler and an umbrella, shouldn't I?" He looked down at his tweed jacket, brown pants, striped tie and loafers and grimaced. "I need a makeover."

"How can you talk about makeovers after yesterday!" I was both furious and aghast.

"I don't know, I should be mad at you, but when you start talking, I can't be," he said.

I felt warm. *Change the subject, Vi.*

"How come you are so totally cool that you know about the Avengers and opera and little French dogs that men could care less about and usually hate?"

"I love your dogs, Violetta," Hugo said.

Mick shot him a steely glance and I choked back a laugh.

"I'm just a totally cool person," he said. "When you get to know me better you won't be so surprised."

I was aware of my cheeks heating up again, Mick's warm body inches away from mine and the irate grumbles of Hugo, vibrating against my other shoulder. He didn't like McGuire at all, not one tiny bit, after he had been accused of trying to stab me to death with a pair of scissors used for trimming my dogs' hair. Hugo was muttering the words "lawsuit" and "false arrest," but we wisely ignored him.

"Let's go, shall we?" I said in an attempt to retain my dignity. I picked up my purse and cape just in time to see Dolly Wilde extend her hands to Roxanne de Winter and pull her out of her chair in a motherly embrace.

"My poor little lamb!" Dolly said to Roxanne and I kid you not, she walked out of the room with Roxanne's weeping blonde face pressed to her matronly shoulder.

"I can't believe it," Hugo said in awe. I was in awe, too. How could the wife and mistress be so fond of each other? In my opera libretto world one of those ladies would have been dead a long time ago.

The buffet was lavish and sumptuous food was enjoyed by many. I didn't have much appetite and waited for a white jacketed waiter to open a fresh bottle of Chardonnay and held up my hand. Unless someone had taken a hypodermic needle and injected cyanide into all the bottles of vino I should be safe.

Everyone else was walking around with loaded plates of curried shrimp, baked brie, and the famed Lobster Newberg eaten on a puff pastry shell. It smelled delicious but I was being paranoid. It would be too easy to put arsenic in the lobster. Since it was drenched in a thick, gooey white cream sauce who would notice a few pounds of arsenic powder mixed in the Alfredo?

Thank God, there were no powdered cookies. In fact there were no cookies anywhere. Dessert seemed to consist of coffee, tea and little fruit tarts. Very prim and proper and what you see is what you get. No powder, no cinnamon, nothing that could have been shaken out of a jar.

I sat drinking wine, watching Hugo mingle with his new groupies. I was tired and wanted to go home. I would finish this glass and go. I longed to talk to Scarlett but she had probably been told not to call me. I saw old man Schwegel inching over in my direction. I sighed and waited.

"Quite a hootenanny," he said.

"Why aren't you playing the bagpipes?"

"I wasn't asked," he said. "I offered but they said no, politely."

"Dolly would never have said no to you," I said.

"It wasn't Dolly, it was those two overstuffed southern drama queens Dolly has protecting her," he said with malice tinged with appreciation.

"Don't you like her sisters?" I asked innocently.

"No, I don't like them, but I admire their vast bosoms and enormous-"

I stood up abruptly. "I'm sorry about the bagpipes, Jerry. Maybe you can play at Mark's memorial service-whenever there is one."

"I already asked about that," he said. "Mrs. Vandermeer is going to let me know."

I breathed a heavy sigh. I didn't want to hear anymore about the vast and enormous mounds of flesh Dolly and her sisters had to offer the planet. I wanted out of here. I didn't want to think about sex.

That hand, that ever present warm hand dropped out of the sky onto my shoulder again.

"Aren't you eating anything, Violetta?" the molten lava voice of Mick McGuire breathed into my ear.

He was stuffing himself on crab cakes and lobster. I gasped. "How do you dare eat this stuff?"

He smiled. "We've been in the kitchens all day," he explained. "We were at the market when the food was bought, in the kitchen when it was prepared and our guys are the waiters, they're doing a great job, don't you think?"

I looked up at a waiter, carefully removing dishes and glasses from a table. He looked up at McGuire, gave a quick thumbs up and nodded.

"The waiters are policemen?"

"Correct."

"And you watched all the food being prepared?"

"Affirmative."

"*Mamma mia*, am I famished. Let me at it," I said and went and got a very large plate full of everything.

Chapter Fifteen

It's better to be looked over than overlooked.

-Mae West

I was working my way through the second puff pastry loaded with Lobster Newberg when Hugo came up with a plate of curried shrimp.

"Try these, Violetta, they are absolutely divine."

I took the plate. "Thank you, Hugo. Are you sitting down?"

He looked thrilled at my offer but shook his spiky head. "I'm delivering shrimp to my ladies," he said and buzzed away. I sat eating seafood waiting for the void in my gut to be filled. I hoped I wouldn't get a massive attack of indigestion from the curry and the rich Newberg sauce. Cream was lactose and I didn't handle it well.

I felt that hand on my shoulder again. I froze with a shrimp between my lips.

"Did you come by car?"

I shook my head and tried to swallow. "No, I'm taking a taxi home tonight."

"No, you're not. I'm giving you a ride when you're ready to go."

I put down my fork. "I'm ready."

Surprise flashed across his rugged face. "You sure?"

"I've eaten enough rich food and drunk enough wine tonight. I'll probably blow up like a dirigible later."

"Let's hope not," he said with a chuckle. He helped me on with my black wool cape. Again that old feeling knocked me for a loop. *Why does his touch have that effect on me?*

She looks a little better tonight. The shock of de Winter's death really wiped her out. And she took it better than I expected when I almost broke the door down. I've got to be careful with her.

We walked to the elevators. Hugo came running up to us.

"Violetta, we're going to the Motel Bar for drinks later," he said. "Want to come? You're welcome, too," he said ungraciously to McGuire.

"Thanks, Hugo," I said, "but I'm tired and I'm going home."

"OK," he said. "Are you working tomorrow?"

"No, I'm off," I said. We rotated weekends in my department.

"Then see you Monday," he beamed and buzzed off. Behind Mick's back he mouthed, *"call me."*

We took the elevator to the ground level and walked through the beautifully appointed lobby, down a flight of stairs where we could hear *That Old Feeling* being sung in the bar and out onto Oak Street.

"Do you go out with Hugo?" he asked carefully.

"Heavens, no! What gave you that idea?"

"He seems awfully fond of you and he's always hanging around. Not to mention the haircut yesterday."

"He's way too young for me," I said. "And I didn't get my haircut, thanks to you."

He had the grace to look ashamed.

"Age isn't everything," McGuire said sagely. "I thought he had a crush on you. He seemed to imply that his feelings were reciprocated."

"They're not," I said, annoyed. "He's just a friend, like a younger brother or something."

"Good," he said. "Then there will be less competition for me."

I gave him a look. "Very funny," I said.

"I'm not joking," he replied.

I felt my stomach lurch. *Desire? Indigestion?*

"I'm parked down here," he said. We walked half a block. We stopped in front of a fire hydrant.

"No ticket for you, I see."

"One of the perks of being a cop, one of the very few perks," he added.

"What else is a perk?"

"You get to accumulate a lot of sick days," he said. He unlocked the door and lifted my cape for me so I could slide in. "But the best perk of all-"

"Yes?"

"The best perk of all is meeting someone like you, Violetta."

"We could have met on Match.com or at the Motel Bar," I said lightly, but my heart was beating faster.

"Not very likely," he said. "I don't go to bars and I gave up Match."

"You just can't sit around and do nothing because you're divorced," I said.

"You just can't sit around and do nothing because you're a widow," he shot back.

"Who said I don't do anything?"

He gave me a quick glance. "That's the word on the street."

"You've been asking my family and my co-workers," I said.

"You're thinking I pumped them for information about you? Wrong. It was all volunteered to me, gladly and willingly. Everyone thinks you should get out more."

"Who's everyone?" I asked suspiciously. "My mother?"

"And your father and your friends like Scarlett and Hugo and Mrs. Wilde."

"She was talking about me?" I was surprised. I didn't think Dolly noticed; she had only focused on the needs of Hieronymus.

"In the nicest way possible," he added.

I switched topics. "Where's Scarlett? Why hasn't she returned my calls?"

"Miss Prendergast and Mr. Lancaster came back downtown for questions today. Miss Prendergast was very cooperative, Mr. Lancaster less so."

"How do you mean?"

"Mr. Lancaster came with an attorney and an attitude. I believe the word *Gestapo* came up a couple of times."

"That's Peter, ready to fight, any time, any day."

"Yes, but is he ready to kill?"

I looked across the road to the lake. A scattering of stars glimmered over the inky water. "I don't know, I don't *know,* Mick," I hit my fist on the dashboard. "Someone is angry enough to kill and I don't know who it is. I'm scared."

"I know you are," he said and pulled off at Belmont and drove up the inner drive past the elegant condos and apartment buildings that faced the lakefront and the park.

"When can I talk to Scarlett?"

"You can talk to her now," he said. "She's home."

"Was she very upset?"

"Actually, she seemed very composed. She stuck to her story about Wilde leaving and then coming back into the Reference Room and trying to put his drunken hands on her."

"Why was she there so late?" I had left by 8:30.

"She had stayed to talk to Peter and then he went to get the car and that's when the incident with Wilde happened."

"Did she tell Peter she had hit Wilde when he drove her home?"

"Apparently not, she told no one," he said.

"Where were the servers for the party?"

"They had already left and the custodians had done most of the cleaning and they were gone, too."

"Something doesn't seem right," I said. "I still don't know why Scarlett stayed so late with Peter."

"That's what we were trying to find out."

He drove down Addison. We passed blocks of fun, hip bars and restaurants, the kind of places I never went to. We stopped at a stoplight right next to Wrigley Field.

"Do you like the Cubs?" I asked.

"I used to go with my ex- but I haven't in a couple of years. Do you like baseball?"

"I used to go with my late husband, he was such a fan, but I haven't gone in five years," I said with a lump in my throat.

"Maybe next summer we can go," he said quietly.

"If we're still speaking," I said.

"If we're still speaking," he smiled. "I predict we will be."

"I'm not clairvoyant," I said. "I can't predict the future."

He put his hand over mine. "I can."

"You mean if I'm not locked up you'll take me to a ballgame?"

"Temper, temper," he said. "God, are you a hothead. Is that part of the Greek and Italian package?"

"I do have a temper and I do get pissed off a lot," I admitted. "You might not want to hang around with a woman who gets emotional."

"I love displays of emotion. My family was very stoic and Irish. You weren't supposed to show any signs of weakness. My grandmother was more fiery and honest about emotions. She was part Italian, too."

"Is she still alive, your grandmother?"

"She sure is, she's 85 and lives not too far away from you in Andersonville."

"Where do you live?" I was curious.

"I thought you'd never ask," he said. "I live in Wicker Park. I bought a condo there after the divorce. It's close to downtown and I like the ethnic mix there."

"Yes, Wicker Park is one of the few neighborhoods that hasn't been completely re-gentrified. Not yet, anyway."

"I know, every time a homeowner sells, the building is knocked down and a very expensive new building is put up. The middle class is getting priced out of neighborhoods near downtown and the lake," he said. "I only want to stay there for a while and then get a home with some room."

"You have plans," I said.

"I have plans to get married again and have children. Don't you?"

"Is this an official investigation?"

He pulled up in front of my house and turned off the car.

"No, this is strictly personal research." He pulled me into his arms and kissed me. I was speechless, breathless and unable to move. His mouth was deliciously warm and wet. His tongue was firm and tasted like peppermints. At first I sat still in absolute frozen paralysis but after a couple of seconds I felt myself responding and melted into his arms. He had amazing muscles and I could feel his body melding into mine. I hadn't been kissed in five years. He felt good, he tasted good, had I no shame at all to be smooching a policeman who still thought I might be capable of obstructing justice?

I was rubbing my hands up and down his strong back in total enjoyment when I felt a lump in the pocket of his jacket. I pulled my mouth away from his probing lips.

"Is that your gun?"

"No, it's my Duncan yo-yo."

"Your what?"

"My yo-yo. I always carry one, it helps me to relax and think things out."

"You're kidding. Then where's your gun?"

"In a shoulder holster. Don't worry, it won't go off."

"I wasn't worried," I breathed into his mouth.

"Good," he said and claimed my lips again in a passionate kiss. We continued this wanton smooch fest for a few more minutes when he stopped his exploration of my mouth to murmur, "you are delectable."

"I'm glad you think so," I murmured.

He was about to lean in again for another kissing session when I suddenly got a rumble in my stomach.

"Would you like to come in for a drink?" I said, moving back and unbuckling my seatbelt.

"Yes, I would, very much," he said. His voice was very deep and thick with emotion. Judging from my reaction to his kiss I guessed the emotion to be lust.

"Then let's go in," I said and opened the car door. I heard a little sigh behind me.

I put the key in the lock and heard barking. My parents had watched the dogs today because they knew I would be home later. Pop must have just walked the little guys home when I called him from the Drake to say I was leaving.

I opened the hall door and Samson and Delilah came bounding out happily to see me. These murders were getting in the way of the amount of quality time I could spend with my dogs. They jumped up at me and then started circling Mick in excitement. They loved company, especially when they could be the center of attention. Mick picked up a tennis ball and started bouncing it. I dropped my cape and purse on a dining room chair and went into the kitchen.

"What would you like to drink?" I asked. "Coffee, tea, beer, wine, Gatorade?"

"Do you have any whiskey?" he was scratching S and D's ears and they were loving it. *I'd like him to scratch my ears.*

I wish she'd come back quickly. I want to kiss her again. Damn, I hope I haven't scared her off. I did grab her without knowing if she wanted to be kissed. But those vibes!

I went into the pantry and came back with a bottle of Pop's Crown Royal. "Is this all right?"

He looked at the bottle. "Perfect."

"Ice?"

"A couple of rocks will do it."

I found a suitable manly whiskey glass and put a couple of ice cubes into it. I poured a couple of fingers, as Sam Spade would say, of Crown Royal into the glass and handed it to Mick.

"Thank you, aren't you going to have anything?"

"I put on the kettle for tea." I rubbed my stomach. "I don't feel so good. The food was very rich."

"And you're an herbal tea and organic food sort of woman, right?"

"Not exactly. I've been known to eat an entire bag of Tootsie Rolls on Halloween. I love all kinds of food, but I'm so used to my mom and dad's fabulous cooking that most restaurant food makes me nervous."

"I'm sure the food was cooked right, some of our guys used to be chefs and went to culinary school. And the Drake Hotel chefs supervised."

He took a swig of the whiskey and coughed. "I'm out of practice, I guess, drinking the hard stuff."

"Do you want some water or more ice?"

"No, I'll be a man and toss this back," he smiled boyishly. My heart flip-flopped. *Should I let him kiss me again?*

She's so pretty. I wish she'd take her hair down. Can I kiss her again?

"So show me a trick," I said.

His green eyes turned emerald and his grin made me break into a sweat.

"What kind, little girl?"

"A yo-yo trick," I said quickly.

He looked disappointed for a second. "Oh yeah, my yo-yo." He put down his glass and took the yo-yo out of his pocket. He stood up and starting expertly spinning it up and down.

"This is a butterfly yo-yo," he told me. It was neon green.

"Very nice," I said. "It matches your eyes." The dogs came up close to check it out but Mick flung it up and around and they beat it.

"That's round the world," he said. He next dropped the yo-yo to the carpet and it walked away from him. "That's walking the dog," he said and then snapped it back up. "And this," he maneuvered the yo-yo up and made the string into a shape, "is the Eiffel Tower." He stopped and smiled like a little boy. I was impressed. *I was in love.*

"Ooh la, la," I said. "You sure are a wealth of hidden talents."

"You should see the rest of them," he said with a grin.

The tea kettle started whistling and I was glad to have an excuse to leave the room. Those green eyes saw way too much.

"Want some tea?" I called into the living room.

"Sure, thank you."

"What kind?"

"Surprise me."

I was deciding between chamomile and peppermint tea when the stomach cramps and the twitching began. I poured out two cups of the chamomile hoping it would settle my stomach but I had to hold on to the kitchen island to steady myself and wait for the pain to subside. *Why did I eat that Lobster Newberg?*

I walked back into the living room and Mick immediately knew something was wrong.

"What's the matter?" he said. "You don't look so good."

I put the teacups down on the coffee table with a thump. The cups rattled because my hands were shaking. "I guess that's why you're a detective, you're so perceptive." I tried to make the words into a joke, but I was clutching my stomach with both hands and grimacing.

Mick was ready to spring into action. "We should go to the hospital right now. Where's your doctor?"

"St. Joseph's," I said, "but I am definitely not going to the hospital! It's just a little gas from the rich food. I will drink this tea and take some Tums and I'll be OK."

He looked at me suspiciously. "I don't know about that. I'll get you the Tums. Where are they?"

I directed him to the top of the refrigerator. He came back with the bottle. He opened it and shook out two tablets on his hand. We both stared at the pink and yellow fruit flavored discs skeptically.

"Well, here goes," I said and bit into the yellow tablet. It tasted chalky and vaguely fruit flavored but I couldn't name a fruit. I tried to pick up the other tablet but my hands were twitching even more and I suddenly got a cramp in my stomach that needed immediate attention. I got up and ran to the bathroom leaving Mick, Samson and Delilah to stare at my mad dash.

There is nothing like buckets of diarrhea when you're trying to be chic and cool and madly sexy. I cursed myself, my stomach and Hieronymus Wilde's mad obsession with Lobster Newberg as I sat on the porcelain throne being sick. I ran the cold water in the sink hoping to drown out my groans of agony and the eruptions that were pouring out of my body.

"Damn, hell and blast!" This could not be happening to me.

There was a gentle rap on the door. "Violetta? What can I do for you?"

"Just get me a new stomach," I groaned.

"I'm going to call your doctor," he said. "Give me his number."

"No wait, I think it's over," I said. I started to stand up but sank back down. I flushed the toilet a couple of times and wet a wash cloth to put on my face. I was ice cold and I seemed to have no control over my hands. They were shaking and twitching and I felt like my legs were doing the same thing. After another minute or two I did stand up, pulled up my hose and managed to walk out of the bathroom.

Mick stood there giving me the once over. "Well?"

"I'm OK, it's passed, and I feel better." On shaky legs I sat down in a vintage 60's bucket chair covered in lime green leather. I did not pick up the cup.

He was watching me intently when his phone rang.

He pulled it out of his pocket. "McGuire, homicide," he said. His entire demeanor immediately changed. "When? Where?" He looked at me. "We'll be there."

"I'll get your coat. We're going to the hospital."

"Why, what's happened?" *The room seemed to be spinning or was it me?*

"Dolly Wilde, Roxanne de Winter and Hugo Haydn have all been admitted into the Northwestern Hospital Emergency Room," he told me quietly. "Some sort of food poisoning is suspected. Do you think you can walk?"

Chapter Sixteen

The less we know the more we suspect.

-Josh Billings

The night was cold and clear and handfuls of tiny flickering stars spotted the sky. I shivered and pulled my cape around me. I felt totally beyond weak.

With Mick's help he got me into the car. Again and again, my hands twitched and I had the sensation of spinning. As Mick drove, he made calls.

"I'll call you, Mr. and Mrs. Aristotle, immediately, if there's any change. She looks OK, but I want to make sure." I could hear their strong voices carrying out of the cell phone. He spoke reassuringly to them and they finally rang off.

We drove in silence. He put on the siren and light and we made it back to Chicago Avenue, two blocks from the Drake Hotel in under 8 minutes. I was scared. I was admitted into the emergency room. I sat on a cold white examining table. A cute young doctor and a very experienced older nurse checked me in. My vitals were taken, along with blood. My blood pressure was a little low but my pulse and breathing were fine. My pupils were a bit dilated. I had no temperature. I felt horrible. I didn't want to be poked anymore. When they asked me if I had kept a stool sample, I broke into laughter and began to vomit. I was put on a hospital bed and transported to another room. Here I found Hugo and Roxanne, their beds pushed close together, holding hands.

"Violetta," Hugo howled. "What has happened to us? Have we all been poisoned, too?" He looked frantic and he was shaking like he was freezing.

"I don't know, maybe it's salmonella or E.coli or maybe the lobster was bad or something," I said. "Let's not get into a panic." Like I wasn't already. "And where's Dolly?"

"Dolly is unconscious and has been admitted to a room in intensive care," Roxanne told me, crying into a lace handkerchief. "It's just terrible." Her lips were trembling and her right eye twitched. *What the hell was happening to us?*

"When did you get sick?"

"We stayed at the party until the end," Hugo said. "We wanted to support Dolly. Roxanne and I were going to share a taxi going home. There were only a few guests left when all of a sudden Dolly began having stomach pains."

"And chest pains," Roxanne added. "We thought she was having a heart attack."

"By the time the paramedics came to take her to the hospital, we were both having the same symptoms," Hugo said. "My stomach was hurting something awful, Violetta. I thought I was going to explode."

"Did you have a major attack of the runs?" I asked.

Roxanne coughed delicately.

"As a mater of fact, we did," she said. "It was awful," she wrinkled her perfect nose and exhaled a dainty breath. "I was very sick." She tried to pat her face with the lace hanky but her hand shook so that she shoved it down into her lap.

"So was I," I said. "How are you feeling now?"

"Better, much better," she said. *I didn't believe her.*

Two doctors came into the room with nurses and other staff. One was very tall and had a bushy beard, he looked like Moses. The other looked like a very young Paul Newman with dazzling blue eyes. Somewhere along the way a few detectives had slipped in and were standing in the back trying to look unobtrusive.

Moses started to speak. "We're glad you got here so quickly, we want to start dispensing activated charcoal right away."

"What's that and what's it for?" I asked.

The nurses came up to us with large containers of a liquid grey substance. It looked like a clear milk carton with a straw. Except this was the vilest looking milk I had ever seen.

"It's a charcoal-carbon based substance and it's been made into a liquid for patients who might have ingested a hazardous substance," he explained, very nicely.

"Like poison or drugs," I said.

"Exactly," he said.

"I don't want to take it," I said. "I feel fine." But I too was starting to twitch again from the cold and fright.

"I'm glad you're feeling fine but there is a chance that you might have ingested something hazardous during the dinner after the- funeral service?" He looked to the detectives for corroboration; they nodded and he continued.

"Have we been poisoned?" Hugo was near tears.

"We don't know yet, everything's been sent to the lab. So- there's no time to waste. You must start drinking the charcoal right now."

I waited for a drum roll or a clap of thunder but instead the nurses came up to us holding the vile looking stuff. A kindly looking nurse came and raised the head of the portable hospital bed. She took off my cape and pushed my sweaty, disheveled hair which had come undone away from my face. When she saw that I was comfortable she came at me with the milk box and the straw. She looked determined. I was reminded of my mother and I didn't want to be a total ass so I let her hold the straw to my lips. I took a tiny sip and gagged. It tasted like cold cigar ash.

"I can't do this," I said and put a trembling hand up to my mouth.

"Of course you can, just take a few sips at a time. Do it quickly, without thinking about it," she was encouraging me. "I'll hold the straw for you. In a few minutes it will be over."

It seemed more like a millennium but in 15 minutes we had ingested most of the charcoal. Roxanne looked as grey as the stuff we drank, Hugo was now freely crying and I was just in the most depressed mood in the world. Most of all I wanted to see McGuire. I wanted to know how we had been poisoned. Hadn't he assured me that the food was bought, prepared, cooked and served by his own hand-picked men? Then how the hell did somebody put something in our food? And why wasn't everybody else poisoned? Why were we four picked out of the crowd? Who had it in for us?

I was still mulling this over when the next attack of diarrhea hit. I felt a punch to the gut and I knew I had to move it. I jumped out of the bed and I was running to the pristine white all-purpose bathroom when I banged into Mick McGuire.

"Violetta!" his grabbed my arms to steady me.

"Out of my way!" I cried. "Hurry!"

He stood back and I bolted in the toilet. I sat there for many, many minutes. My beautiful Emma Peel skirt was sagging and covered with little bits of charcoal and my panty hose had many snags in them. Finally I got up, flushed again and looked into the mirror. I almost fainted. I looked like the Wicked Witch of the West. I was practically green and my hair had come undone and was laying about my sweaty face in snake-like tendrils. I stuck out my tongue and saw that it was black. Heaven help me, I was turning into a *strega*, like in the old spooky Italian witch stories I used to beg my mother to read to me when I was little. All I needed was a broom and a black cat.

I splashed water on my face and took down the rest of my hair. I always had a hair tie in my purse and I wanted to tie my hair back and get it off my face. I needed my purse. I would leave this throne room made of ceramic and make myself presentable and then leave. Throwing open the door dramatically I observed the frozen looks of Hugo, Roxanne, Mick McGuire, the nurses and the two remaining detectives. I was ready to sing a gypsy aria and give them a little leg like *Carmen* or *Azucena* from *Trovatore*, but instead I threw my head back and walked proudly across the room. There I opened my purse, found the hair tie and pulled all my hair back into a severe ponytail. I put on lip gloss; I spritzed some 4711 cologne on my neck and wrists. I took a deep breath. I was ready.

"I would like to go home now," I announced to the room. "Would someone get me a taxi?"

"We'll drive you home." McGuire said in an official voice. "*After* the doctors say it is all right for you to leave." He was challenging me; I could tell by the way he thrust out his jaw. I was not to be daunted.

"I am checking myself out of this hospital immediately," I said loftily, hoping I wouldn't soil my pants while I made an exit worthy of Bette Davis. I began to move, feeling a little woozy and wooden but then Pop appeared at the door and my heart began to sing with love.

"Violetta!" he cried. "What has happened to you, *koukla mou?"*

I crossed the room in three quick strides. "Pop! Pop! Take me home, I want to get out of here." I know I sounded immature and panicky but I didn't care. Pop was here and he would take care of me.

He put his arm around my shoulders. "*Koukla*, we'll go home. Anything you say." One thing about Pop he could assume leadership when needed. As a new U.S. citizen he had volunteered to be in the army and went to Vietnam. He had run his restaurant for many years with a kind but very firm hand. He was not afraid of doctors or the police.

The doctor from toxicology who looked like Paul Newman met us in the hall.

"Your friends are spending the night for observation," he said pleasantly. "Why don't you, too? This way we can be sure you won't have any reactions."

My dad looked at me. I shook my head vigorously.

"My daughter wants to come home," he said firmly. "My wife and I will watch her all weekend at our house. We'll take good care of her."

The blue eyes checked us out and made a decision that we didn't look helpless. He took a card out of his pocket.

"Here's my number," he said. "And my pager. Call me if anything changes."

I wish I wasn't standing there in a sweaty and crumpled dress, reeking of charcoal and the bathroom.

When I finally meet a cute doctor, I look like hell. I sighed.

"Thank you, Dr.-" I looked at the card. "Randell. I will call you if I need anything. But right now, all I want to do is go home and sleep."

"Good idea," he agreed pleasantly. "But you will look in on her during the night?"

"Every hour," my father said. "She'll be in good hands."

I looked at my father's big, tanned hands. I felt better all ready.

Mick McGuire was waiting for us at the elevator. I had a signed a release paper and I had politely declined to leave the hospital in a wheelchair. I wanted to walk and most of all, I wanted to breathe fresh air.

He got into the elevator with us. My father greeted him like an old friend.

"What's going on here?" Dad asked. "When will it end?"

I had to admit, Mick looked terrible. He looked grim and tired and his green eyes were tinged with red. He had probably slept little all week and now tonight had been a fiasco for him and his people.

"It's going to end soon," he said carefully. "Don't repeat this, but we are close to making an arrest."

"You are?" I finally acknowledged him. "Care to give me a hint?"

He shook his head. "I'm not at liberty to say."

God, he sounded right out of Perry Mason. How formal we've become.

"Well, you'd better make it soon, before we're all dead," I snapped. I was acting like a **B**, but I didn't care. My father looked at me in surprise. I was usually not this rude but fear and puke and the memory of my bashed in back door had made me crabby.

"How is Mrs. Wilde?" my dad asked.

"She has regained consciousness and is doing remarkably well. Whatever caused your illness has passed through you very quickly," Mick answered.

I felt my stomach with queasy hands. "I'll say it passed through us quickly."

The elevator opened. Pop said, "I'll go get the car. Will you stay with her?"

"Absolutely," McGuire said.

I stood mute and defiant.

"Why are you so mad at me?" he inquired softly.

I felt a jolt in my guts again, whether from the charcoal or his nearness, I wasn't sure.

"You told me we were safe, you told me we could eat the food. I believed you and now look what happened to us. We could have been killed." *It's not his fault someone hates librarians. I'm being unfair.* "Yesterday you break my door down and pull a gun on a friend of mine who was going to cut my hair, for God's sake. Today, when I'm in real danger-" I stopped. He looked stricken. I had said enough.

"I am truly sorry, if I knew anything was going to happen to you, Violetta, I never would have let you go to the memorial service," he said. "I don't want you or your friends to suffer."

He looked as miserable as I felt.

"I'm sorry I got mad," I said. "I hate being sick and I hate hospitals."

"I know you do," he said. "I'm sorry."

I shut my eyes, trying to block out the vision of Siegfried in this very hospital.

"Truce?" he held out his hand. He had tiny red-gold hairs on his hands and knuckles. So many red-heads around here lately. Wilde, Hugo, Scarlett and now Mick.

I sighed. I was too tired to fight anymore. "Truce." We shook hands and then he pulled me in his arms.

"You're going to be OK," he murmured into my ear. "You are not going to leave your parents' house until I am completely sure that this nightmare is all over."

It felt good to have his arms around me again; it felt good to have someone other than my parents care for me. I sank into his embrace and took a deep breath. I sniffed his lime cologne and held on to him for dear life. He rubbed my back with tender fingers. I wanted to kiss him again and make him taste the charcoal on my tongue. It would be part punishment-part pleasure. I was practically having a pleasant S&M fantasy but then my dad pulled up in the car and my moment of wild mental carnal abandon was over.

Chapter Seventeen

The only way to get rid of a temptation is to yield to it.

-Picture of Dorian Grey, Oscar Wilde

The next morning I awoke with an enormous hangover and an enormous appetite. I assumed the quasi hangover was from the food, the drink and being stuffed with a pound of charcoal ashes. Also from sitting on a toilet feeling like an avalanche had run through my intestines. I got up cautiously and found the floor stayed put under my feet. Samson and Delilah were taking their morning nap. I looked at the clock. 10:30am.

Last night I had sat up until the wee hours talking to my mom and dad about the terrible occurrences of the week. I think they wanted to make sure that I wasn't going to die on them, so we drank chamomile tea, ate oyster crackers and talked. I sent my dad to bed at midnight because I knew he was going to get up at 4:30 to get ready to go the restaurant. My mom and I stayed up quite a bit later, until almost 4 a.m.

I felt badly because I had ruined their sleep and I knew my mom had a busy day of lessons. I opened the bedroom door and heard a tenor struggling through *Nessun Dorma* from the opera *Turandot.* How appropriate, I thought. *No one sleeps*, the man was singing. He was trying to guess a riddle to save his head from being chopped off and to win the princess' love. Pretty hokey drama, but it still worked both musically and dramatically. Puccini knew what he was doing.

I took a shower and inspected my teeth. They still looked grey from the charcoal. I kept brushing and brushing. *Out, damn spots.* I came down the stairs with Samson and Delilah at my heels. My mother was just letting her student out. When she saw me she gave me a big hug.

"How are you, darling? Hungry?"

"Ma," I said, "I could eat a horse."

"I'll see if I have one in the freezer," she said and took me into the kitchen.

I was in the middle of bacon and eggs, Greek toast, coffee and cranberry juice when the doorbell rang.

"Another student?"

"Not for a while," my mom said, looking at the clock. She went to answer the door and I dashed into the bathroom to check my hair and face. What if it was Mick?

It wasn't.

"Scarlett! At last! I've been trying to reach you!" We embraced and I gave her a quick once over. She looked tired and despondent.

"It's been hell this week," she said and gratefully accepted a cup of coffee from my mother. "Your friend was over early this morning quizzing me about everything again."

"McGuire?"

"That's the man. He seems to think Peter and I were somehow responsible for your getting sick last night. He implied that we smuggled ourselves into the Drake Hotel and laced your food with- whatever it was that made you sick." She sighed. "This is never going to end. I wish they would arrest us and get it over with."

"You don't mean that!" I choked on my toast. "You don't want to be charged with a pseudo-murder."

"Whose pseudo murder? Wilde is dead. If I didn't deal him the fatal blow, I contributed to his death."

I suddenly realized she was feeling remorse. "Don't feel bad, Scarlett, you were telling the truth." *Wasn't she?*

"Not entirely. I told the police that I was in the department talking to Peter and then Peter left for the car and Wilde came in unexpectedly. It's not true. Peter and I had quarreled and he left me. I had an assignation with Wilde. We had set it up earlier in the day. He said he had something to tell me that was important."

"And what was it?" I was holding my breath.

"He never told me," she admitted. "He was drunk and acting like a fool. He did try to lunge at me, Violetta, he really did. He did try to kiss me. I was disgusted and hit him with the stick before I knew what I had done. It happened so quickly."

"I believe you," I said. "I know you're not a violent person."

"I believe you're wrong," Scarlett said. "I almost killed a man Monday. I am capable of violence, Violetta." She clenched and unclenched her strong hands. "We all are. I learned that. He might have died from the blow to his head, but we'll never know now."

Thank God for that. It could save her from prison.

She read my thoughts. "I know- if he hadn't been poisoned I would be awaiting trial for manslaughter or murder. It's unbelievable."

My mother brought her a plate of eggs and toast.

"Thank you, Sophia; I haven't been able to eat all week."

The doorbell rang again.

"Grand Central Station," I sang out and threw crusts of toast to my pooches.

My mother started for the door again.

"Sit, Mom, I'll get it." I headed for the door. *Let her rest, God knows I've upset her enough this week.*

I sensed his presence before I actually saw him standing at the door. His red hair was shining in the sun and he was wearing a fringed suede jacket, very Wyatt Earp-ish. I was surprised by his choice of clothing. If people were dogs then Mick McGuire was an Irish setter this morning, big, energetic, lanky and very friendly. I was hoping today to act more like a French Poodle than a Pit Bull. *But the day was young.*

"Good morning," I said. "Have you come to sell Girl Scout cookies?"

I saw him looking at my Illini t-shirt and my hair that I had tied in two pigtails at the sides of my head. I had fuzzy Elmo slippers on my feet. At least this morning I was wearing pants.

"No, tickets to the Policeman's Ball," he smiled. "You look like a little girl." He tugged at one of my pigtails.

"I am a little girl," I said demurely. I looked down at his feet. "Wow! Real cowboy boots! How tall does that make you now, 7 feet?"

"About six foot ten, I reckon," he said.

"Very cool. You look terrific." We stood in the doorway absolutely beaming at each other. I wanted to run my fingers through his thick, wavy hair.

"I got the boots in Denver, when I was visiting my brother," he told me. He coughed. "Is it OK if I come in? I don't want to disturb your family."

Like hell you don't. Uh-oh, it's starting. The interrogation will commence.

She was looking like a sugar plum until I asked her if I could come in. I hope she doesn't get all defensive on me right away.

He followed me through the house. "Detective McGuire," I announced in the doorway and went to finish my breakfast. He waited in the doorway and my mother, Scarlett and the dogs blinked at the red-haired cowboy. My mother recovered first.

"Come in, Mick, nice to see you," she cooed, just like it was a social call. "How about I fix you some eggs and bacon?"

"Thank you Mrs. Aristotle, but I've already eaten. But I would love a cup of your delicious coffee."

What a suck up.

My dogs jumped up to be patted. Scarlett sat quietly drinking coffee.

"Hello, again," she said lightly. "So we meet again so soon."

"Hello, Miss Prendergast," he said, very politely. "I'm sorry to interrupt your breakfast but I wanted to drop by and see how Vio- Miss Aristotle was feeling this morning." *We were all procedure now.*

"I'm feeling as fit as a fiddle," I told him. "Outside of a massive headache I'm doing fine. How is Dolly?"

"Mrs. Wilde is doing so well that she will be going home later today. She insists on leaving the hospital. Her two sisters will be there to look after her and also a nursing assistant for a couple of days. She made a quick recovery."

"How about Roxanne and Hugo?" I asked. "I was about to call the hospital."

"They were discharged this morning. They are also feeling much better today."

"Thank God!" my mother cried and made the sign of the cross.

Scarlett and I exchanged looks of relief. "I'm so happy to hear that," I said. "Did you ever find out what was in the food that made us have stomach cramps and get sick?"

He was drinking coffee and looking relaxed. At my question he put down the cup and got all official again.

"Yes, I'll get to that in a minute. First I'd like to ask you if you ever saw Mrs. Wilde with her purse last night?"

"Her purse?" I was mystified.

"Yes, her purse, handbag- it appears to have gone missing."

"It was stolen?" Scarlett asked.

"A police report has been filed. But at this point we don't know if it was stolen or if it got misplaced in the confusion of her getting sick. The hotel of course is looking into it."

"I never saw her with a purse last night," I said, thinking furiously. "I saw her in the receiving line at the memorial and later sitting at a table during the buffet dinner. I didn't see her coat or purse. I assumed they were in the coatroom or in the car or with her sisters."

"Thank you," he said.

"So what made my daughter sick?" My mother was waiting, poised on the edge of her seat. So was I.

"The lab tests have confirmed that you all had a case of poisoning by strychnine. It appears someone sprinkled rat poison into your food."

The room became so still I could hear the pounding of my heart.

"Rat poison? In our food? That's unbelievable! Why didn't we taste it?" I had risen to my feet and was waving my arms around like a mad conductor.

"I bet it was in the Lobster Newberg," my mother said. "That thick sauce will disguise anything. What a monster to try to poison my baby." She was near tears.

"Actually we think it was put into the curried shrimp that some of you ate," he explained. "The curry powder would mask the tartness of the strychnine."

"I ate rat poison," I said. "I can't believe it."

"How many shrimp did you eat? Do you remember?" Mick asked.

"I think I ate seven, they were delicious."

"*Mamma mia*," my mother gasped.

"Why did Dolly get sicker than the rest of us?" I felt my hands shaking again, this time from shock.

"I believe Mrs. Wilde," here he whipped out the infamous BlackBerry, punched a few buttons and then read- "ate about 24 shrimp. She said she simply adores seafood."

"So she passed out from the amount of strychnine in her system?" I needed facts and details.

"Actually what made her pass out actually saved her," McGuire said. "She had taken two diazepam-Valium, before the memorial service because she was feeling nervous and stressed. The Valium interacted with the wine to make her unconscious but it also stopped the convulsions. You remember how you and Mr. Haydn and

Mrs. de Winter were all shaking when you got to the hospital?"

"It was from the rat poison?" I asked.

"Strychnine causes convulsions. It was a good thing you took the activated charcoal immediately upon arriving at the hospital. It's a miracle that you are all doing so well," he said.

"I didn't think policemen talked about miracles, only procedures," I said.

"This policeman believes," he said and gave me a look. I felt liquid inside. I didn't think my guts could take anymore.

Chapter Eighteen

People never notice anything.

-Holden Caulfield

McGuire finished his coffee, got a brief phone call, said "where did you find it?" and left in a New York minute. I walked him to the door but he only said, "call you later," and flew out the door. I watched him and his hand tooled cowboy boots stomp down the front steps without a backward look. I was miffed. He had just given me the big melting lover boy look and then had vamoosed pretty darn quick.

Scarlett and I lingered over our toast while my mother coaxed a timid soprano through *Caro nome* from *Rigoletto.* While no Maria Callas by the time she was done the young lady sounded almost ready for a night at the Met or La Scala. My mother worked miracles with the voice.

The phone rang. I picked it up without looking at the caller I.D. *Who cared at this point?*

"This is Lois Dalton Vandermeer, may ah pah-leese speak to Violetta?"

"This is she," I said dutifully. I wanted to slam down the phone. I mouthed "Vandermeer," at Scarlett. She leaned over and tried to listen in at the phone with me.

"Ah wanted to call and ask you how are yah feeling? Ah am so sorry to hear about your being indisposed," Mrs. Vandermeer drawled.

"I'm feeling better," I said. "Thank you for calling."

"Ah wanted to ask if you would be coming into work Monday," her voice was cordial.

"Of course, I will," I said. *Why wouldn't I?*

"Ah see," she said. "Mrs. de Winter has applied for a short leave of absence. Ah wanted to call and ask if you wanted to do the same."

Instant paranoia. *Was she trying to get rid of me?*

"No, I have no intention of applying for a leave. I'm quite recovered. Thank you for asking."

"It was mah pleasure," she drawled and hung up.

"She wants to know if I'm taking a leave of absence. Apparently Roxanne is," I said.

"Is Hugo?"

"Hugo is indestructible," I said. "He's only 22."

"And you're an antique at 32, I suppose," Scarlett sighed. She was 42.

"I am a widow, a department head and I've found two dead bodies in two days," I said loftily. "I am somebody." I put my head down on the kitchen table. "And I have a headache."

"Go back to bed," she said kindly. "Do you still want to go visit Dolly tomorrow?"

"Yes, let's go and visit her. We can bring her flowers and chocolate, she's fond of both. I don't want to wait too long; it will be a sign of our strength and support to go visit her."

"Will her sisters even let us in?" Scarlett mused.

"They had better, dahling," I drawled. "Or we might have to fight our way in."

"As long as we don't have to fight our way out," Scarlett said.

The rest of the day I slept, walked the dogs, and helped my mother make manicotti. I don't know why my parents aren't both 300 pounds, they love to eat, but I guess like me they keep very busy and have good metabolisms. I kept waiting for another phone call or even a visit from Mick but I heard nothing. I wanted to call Hugo and Roxanne but decided to wait until tomorrow. Hugo would gossip for hours and Roxanne- I wasn't sure if I would be invading her privacy.

I slept the night but kept having dreams about rat-eating shrimp wearing cowboy boots which began to become Dali-esque by dawn. I got up very early, took a shower and washed my hair and made French toast for my parents. Dad was off today and he always spent Sundays with my mom. They loved to hang out together.

When they came downstairs together looking like newlyweds I had the coffee brewing and the griddle hot. They were impressed.

"Look! She's going to cook for us," my mother was beaming.

"I wish you'd quit this library business and work with me," my dad said. "Aristotle and Aristotle, we could become famous."

"Yes, and get a show on the Food Network and become the next Emeril and Julia Child," I said.

"She was a nice lady," Pop said. He had met her on a tour of Chicago long ago. She had eaten at his restaurant. He loved her Coq au vin and she loved his waffles and spinach pie. "Why not come and work with me?"

I was feeling tempted. Maybe if I stayed at the library I wouldn't be around to enjoy Pop's waffles or Mom's manicotti much longer. And yet, I didn't want to turn my back on my career. I loved books and I love libraries and I couldn't imagine spending my days without them.

"Thanks, Pop, can I wait a few years for that?"

He looked disappointed but then smiled, showing big, strong white teeth. He was the perfect Zorba the Greek for this century.

"Of course, *koukla.*" I was always his little doll.

My mother and father raved about my French toast, (it was passable) praised the coffee, (it was OK) and made a big deal over the honey butter I had whipped up for them (my specialty with a secret ingredient).

"We hate to leave you but we're going to church," my mother said. One week they hit the Catholic church; the next Sunday the Greek church. When I was a kid I went to Catholic school during the week and Greek school on Saturdays until I rebelled and insisted I go to the public high school. Surprisingly my parents went along with that.

"Sure you don't want to join us?" My father would have loved me to go, and I hated to disappoint him but I didn't feel like praying. I was still too numb.

"Next week, I promise," I said. They both kissed me like they were going on an ocean cruise and left me and Samson and Delilah to relax.

But I couldn't rest; I was full of energy today. I cleaned the kitchen, tried playing tunes from *South Pacific* on the piano for a while and walked the dogs twice. Rummaging through my old closet I found a very nice Elvis t-shirt with the words "legendary" in gold under his crooning face. That would go nicely with my black cashmere cardigan, pearls, gaucho pants and knee high black suede boots. I was visiting someone who was both ill and bereaved and I didn't want to look too flashy. Black was best in these situations.

The bell rang and Scarlett was at the door. I put my pooches in the kitchen with a couple of rawhide chews to amuse them and then I headed out.

"How are you, today?" Scarlett said. We hugged quickly and she kissed my cheek.

"I'm feeling a lot better; it's amazing how good I feel."

"I wish you'd take some time off of work," she said.

"That's what my parents say," I sighed. "But I feel I should go in."

"I can keep an eye on things until you feel like coming back."

I squeezed her arm. "I know you can, it's not that. It's just that the longer I stay away, the more I'm afraid I will never want to go back. And then where will I be? Without a job and without a home if I don't make the mortgage payments." *And without a life.*

"I know. It would be lovely to be independently wealthy," she sighed. "And not have to work at all."

"Wouldn't you be bored?" I looked for her car and didn't see it.

"Peter's giving us a lift," she said. "And no, I wouldn't be bored. I have many alternative career plans."

Peter Lancaster was standing next to his ancient Mercedes and opened the doors for us with a flourish.

"Mademoiselles, je suis enchantée de vous voir."

"I'm enchanted to see you, too, Peter," I said, but I was shocked at his appearance. He looked haggard and he had lost some weight. His wild Beethovian locks had been cut short and without his hair he looked less imposing and older.

Surely Peter wasn't going to visit Dolly?

He read my thoughts as he started the car. "Scarlett and I are going to an antiques show after your visit, so I said I'd drive you ladies. I hope you don't mind?" He looked anxious and I realized that the two of them had been going through extreme hell this week.

"No problem, Peter, thanks for the ride." He headed south for Dolly's gold coast condo. "Oh my!" I said, suddenly in a panic. "I forgot to get flowers!"

"We can stop at Trader Joe's, take a right on Grace Street," Scarlett said. Peter meekly complied with her wishes.

In the parking lot she said, "you stay here and rest, Violetta, I'll get the flowers. I also forgot the chocolate."

I complied with her wishes, too. Scarlett was a good leader. *Maybe I should let her take over the department for a while.*

"So where do you stand right now, Peter," I asked, "with the police investigation?"

"After two days of being bullied and tyrannized by the local *polizia* we have reached a mutual understanding," he said.

"Meaning?"

"They don't think I killed Wilde and de Winter anymore and I don't think they're total idiots."

"How about the *Gestapo*?"

He had the grace to smile. "I got pretty worked up when I was being questioned. Mostly because I was afraid for Scarlett. That swine, Wilde, molesting her like he did. If I had been there I would have killed him."

"I hope you didn't tell the police that," I said. "And why don't they suspect you anymore?"

"They wouldn't tell me, but since Scarlett and I weren't at the memorial service Friday night, that let us out of the poisoning. And I guess something happened yesterday that throws new light on who did the deadly deeds."

"I see." But I didn't see. Who hated Wilde so much that he or she killed him? And why was Mark de Winter so brutally butchered? It just didn't make sense.

Scarlett returned to the car with a beautiful bouquet of roses and a box of Belgian chocolates.

"I hope her two wicked stepsisters let us in," I said.

"I called and told them we were coming," Scarlett assured me. "They said it was lovely of us to come and see poor Dolly."

Scarlett was good at details. Why not take a leave and let her run things for awhile? I would love to go with my parents to see the cousins in Greece. *Maybe a nice cruise around the islands?*

Poor Dolly was looking remarkably well for herself, I thought as we entered her three bedroom condo with two balconies overlooking the lake in the Gold Coast. I stopped in surprise when I saw Hugo, cozily sitting among the sisters, drinking tea and eating muffins. He had brought a beautiful spray of orchids. "Hi, Violetta and Scarlett," he said happily. *How he loved to be in the thick of things.*

"Hi, Hugo," I said. "Feeling better?" The way he was chowing down I assumed he had made a full recovery.

I looked around at Dolly's beautiful home. How two librarians could afford this lavish place was beyond me, but then I remembered all the money Wilde had made after selling his patent to Microsoft. He must have made a fortune for their home was decorated with enormous Persian carpets, Art Nouveau furniture and contemporary paintings and sculptures. I remember Hieronymus saying he liked to support the arts and he and Dolly had gone to New York frequently to visit art galleries, trying to discover the next Basquiat or Warhol. One of the pictures on the wall *was* a Warhol and I was impressed. I wonder how much money he had left to Dolly.

The widow was lying on an ebony leather *chaise longue* swaddled in cashmere wraps. She was wearing a ruffled mauve peignoir trimmed in ivory lace and its opulence did not match her granny glasses and flat page boy grey-blonde hair. She was looking a bit thinner and paler but greeted us energetically and with affection. Her eyes were bright and wide with excitement and she had been carefully made up with pink blush and eye shadow to match her gown.

"Scarlett, Violetta! How lovely of you to come see me," she said.

Why Granny, what big eyes you have! Was Dolly enjoying her new-found notoriety and freedom?

We both leaned over and air kissed her cheek. The two dyed blonde dragons Daphne and Delores were standing by watching our every move. Daphne was wearing pink satin Capri lounge pants with a cashmere sweater emblazoned with rhinestone butterflies. Delores was a tad more sedate in a puce velvet hostess gown, the kind you used to see in Doris Day movies. I was entranced.

"Flowers and chocolate, how kind," Dolly gushed. She stuck her pink nose into the bouquet of roses, inhaled and sneezed. "Isn't this a terrible thing to have happened?" She sat up and tried to rearrange her covers. Immediately her sisters started fussing over her. After a minute of pulling and pushing she was ready for speech.

"Why did someone try to poison you, dear Violetta? And poor, poor Roxanne. And dear Hugo," she blew him a kiss, he blew one back. "It doesn't make sense."

"No, not to me either," I mused. "Unless someone has a vendetta against librarians?"

"Who doesn't like librarians?" Hugo asked incredulously.

"Everyone loves us, dear Hugo," Dolly said, "but I believe there are some twisted, wounded souls in the world. Some people for whom there would be no motive at all. Just senseless killings. Like poor Mark, that quiet, gentle man, his death was ghastly."

"It was," Scarlett agreed. We all sat for a moment in silence. Scarlett changed the subject and I was grateful. "I suppose now you won't be going on your cruise?"

"Certainly not!" Daphne interjected. "We still plan to go."

"Dolly needs the rest and ocean air even more than before," Delores said. "We leave next week. We are even trying to talk Hugo into joining us." He smiled in delicious enjoyment of his dilemma. *Should he join the old babes for a romp around Cape Horn?*

I could see Hugo tango-ing with the Andrews Sisters. *Why not?*

"I hope you have a wonderful time," I said. The doorbell rang. More visitors?

Daphne minced out of the room in her pink marabou trimmed kitten heel slippers. I thought she would make a great drag queen. Maybe Daphne and Delores were really men and they had come to avenge Wilde's philandering by killing him and everyone else who had gotten in Dolly's way. It was a good plot but it didn't explain why Dolly had been poisoned. I was turning this over in my mind when Daphne came back in the room with Mick McGuire and another detective. I sat up very straight in my chair. Had he been following me?

"Mrs. Wilde," he said pleasantly. "Ladies?" He nodded at us courteously. "Mr. Haydn." Mick's eyes missed nothing, the flowers, the cozy tea and scones, my gaucho pants. "This is Detective Halliday," he waved a hand in the silent man's direction. I wanted to shout out "I'm New Year's Day!", but I put a lid on myself. I wondered if I was developing a touch of mental Tourette's.

"I'm sorry to bother you," he said, "but I need to ask you a few questions." He was holding a large book bag, like an over aged school boy.

"Of course," Dolly said. "Sit down, won't you?" She was craning her neck up to look at the giant. No one had the right to be that tall. I saw he was wearing his brown loafers and tweeds and looked like an underpaid policeman again and not Wyatt Earp. I looked for his gun but I guessed it was under his jacket.

Hmmm, I wonder if he takes the gun off when he makes love. I'll never find out.

She looks way too innocent today. I'll probably never get a chance to kiss her again. Elvis, pearls and what are those pants she's wearing? She looks ready for a bullfight.

"Would you like some tea?" Daphne asked. She was eyeing McGuire with interest. She was the babe of the trio and she was giving him a well-practiced eye. Her sweater had a deep v-neck and when she leaned over to pour the tea she exposed her double D's with great skill. She was as busty as me but she flaunted it better.

"Have you come to tell me that you have discovered who did away with my darling Hieronymus?" Dolly raised a lace handkerchief to her eyes.

"We're still working on that ma'am," he said. He took a sip of tea. The delicate Limoges teacup looked incongruously small in his enormous hand. "Actually I've come to talk about your handbag."

"Handbag?" Dolly intoned. "My handbag?" She was no Lady Bracknell but she was doing a good job of sounding regally confused.

"We didn't want to upset you, Dolly, but I'm afraid your purse is missing," Delores said.

"I didn't notice it was gone," Dolly said, bewildered. "I gave you my keys before the service, remember, Delores?"

"Yes and your cell phone, too. You didn't want to be bothered holding a purse."

"Where did you put your purse?" McGuire asked.

Dolly turned to Daphne. "Where did I put it, Daffy?" I choked on tea.

The big man gave me a look. *Behave.*

The hell I will. I smiled sweetly back at him.

"I didn't check it with your coat. Did I give it to you to hold, Dee?"

Delores shook her head. "I can't remember."

Great. Three dumb blondes.

"Have you found it, yet?" Daphne said, leaning forward. *Please, no more cleavage.*

McGuire picked up the book bag. "That's what I wanted to talk to you about," he said. He opened the bag and pulled out a large plastic zip-lock pouch. Encased inside was a black purse. He held it up in front of him. "Is this yours, Mrs. Wilde?"

Dolly peered at the pouch. “I think so; can I take a closer look?”

He walked over and held the bag right under her nose. “It’s a black leather purse, with the Gucci logo, probably 5 years old. On the flap engraved in the leather are the initials D.W.”

Scarlett and I exchanged glances. *They had mislaid a Gucci bag?*

“Is there a red satin heart embroidered inside in the lining?” she asked. “When we bought the bag in Italy years ago, the embroidery was a special service that came with every bag. Hieronymus insisted I get a heart because I was so loved.” She sniffled into her hanky. I thought I was going to be sick. I picked up my teacup and drained it too quickly. A stray tea leaf tickled the back of my throat and I started to cough.

Mick shot me another glance. *Quit it; no theatrics here.*

I stuck my nose up in the air at him. *Screw you, buddy.* I was getting into one of my moods again. He had that effect on me and I hated it.

“Yes, there is a red heart inside,” he said.

“Then it’s mine! Where did you find it?” she asked. She held out her hand for the bag but he did not give it to her. *What was up with that?*

“It was turned into the concierge at the Drake Hotel last night. It took them a while to realize that you were the lady who had been taken to the hospital. There appears to have been much confusion after you became ill.”

“I’m so glad someone was honest and turned in my bag,” Dolly said. “Hieronymus insisted on buying it for me after he sold his invention,” she confided. “I would never have bought such an expensive handbag, but he said to me, *let's live it up, Dolly*, and so we did." She sniffled again. "May I have it back now, please? I'd like my own powder and lipstick."

McGuire slowly shook his head. "I'm sorry but that isn't possible. The contents of your bag have been sent to the crime lab and the bag itself will be used for evidence. When the concierge opened your bag to see who it belonged to, packets of powder were discovered. The powder has been identified as a strychnine-based rodent poison."

We all gasped and began to speak.

"There were also traces of arsenic found in the lining of your purse," he continued, ignoring our protests. "Dolly Wilde, I have a warrant for your arrest for the murder of Hieronymus Wilde and the attempted murders of Roxanne de Winter, Hugo Haydn and-" he did not look at me, "Violetta Aristotle. I am not going to read you your rights because we are not going to question you now or take you in for questioning. We are waiting for the doctor to come and see you later today and tell us when you may be moved."

Now we were all speechless. Except for Dolly, who had half risen up off her recliner, cried, "no, no, it isn't true!" and then fell on the floor in a dead faint. Pandemonium ensued. Her sisters rushed to Dolly's side while giving McGuire looks that could kill. The silent detective Halliday exited the apartment. Scarlett went into the bathroom to get a wet towel (always the Girl Scout!) and to see if they had any smelling salts, Hugo was standing frozen to the floor and I took the opportunity to walk around the living room, picking up photographs and checking out the artwork.

I saw a photograph that made my eyes widen with shock. It was Hieronymus as a very young man, possibly an undergraduate, dressed in a fencing costume. He was very thin and had even more hair but there was no mistaking who it was. I stared at the picture for a while and felt a jolt of recognition. I picked up the silver frame and without a word, dropped it into my purse. I was afraid that Mick had gotten it all wrong.

Chapter Nineteen

Elementary, my dear Watson.

-Basil Rathbone, as Sherlock Holmes.

After a heart stopping minute Dolly revived but then became quite hysterical and burst into tears. While Delores bathed Dolly's head in ice water and eau de cologne (just like in a Victorian melodrama) Daphne dropped the sex kitten act and turned on Mick with all the ferocity of a wildcat.

"How dare you arrest my sister for something she hasn't done! Why Dolly couldn't hurt a fly, she has always been the most tender-hearted of souls," Daphne shrieked at him. "What's the matter with the police department? Why can't they- you-" she spat at Mick, "find out who really killed her husband? Is this what we get for our tax dollars? Ineptitude?" She had turned as pink as her sweater and her massive bust was heaving up and down. Next, she would need the paramedics. I was proud of her for making McGuire squirm. *You go girl, with your bad self.*

"We have followed every lead," McGuire said quietly.

"Followed it up the wrong tree!" Daphne shouted. "And my sister is too sick to go anywhere to answer questions. If you move her, we'll sue your big red-headed ass."

Wow. Keep it up, sistah. I was ready to get Daphne a job with *Dog, the Bounty Hunter.*

"Now, Miss, please," he said. "I'm only..." (*he's going to say it!)* doing my job."

I choked back another laugh. Mick turned to me with a scowl but then the paramedics arrived and the doctors started pouring in. First Dolly's own medicine man that lived in the building, then two old geezers who said they were doctors and who lived on Astor Street a block away, and then the toxicology doctor, the movie star look-a-like appeared. We had been asked to remain, so Scarlett, Hugo and I sat very quietly in the back of the room sipping tepid tea

Daphne continued her rants until Dolly had been sufficiently resuscitated enough to be moved to her bedroom for a rest. Delores, Daphne and the tox doc went into the bedroom with her and shut the door behind them. I wondered if we would have to sit here all day and watch people inhale oxygen. After 20 minutes the paramedics and doctors left, a nurse arrived and a couple of uniformed officers stood waiting in the hall for directions.

McGuire was impressive, I have to admit. He had kept his cool under Daphne's onslaught and now was giving orders with complete control. His rugged, no, now I thought it handsome, face looked very impassive and inscrutable. I gathered from the remarks being made that Dolly would remain at home until she was allowed to be brought in for questioning. The nurse would stay; also the two cops would park it outside in the hallway. They were for "protection," but I bet they were put there by McGuire to make sure Dolly wasn't spirited away in the dead of night and taken on an ocean cruise. Also I wondered if they would come back with a warrant to search for more poisons. I think they would be disappointed, if they did.

Finally, the detective called Halliday told us we could go.

Scarlett was busy ringing Peter on her cell phone as we walked to the elevator.

"Peter, darling, are you there?" she said. She listened for a while. "I'll tell you all about it in the car," she said, looking at the officers waiting in the hall. "Are you parked in front?"

We walked outside. The sun had started to poke through the clouds. The lake smelled like fish today and something else- it smelled like winter. Soon the leaves would be swept away and we would be engulfed in months of snow, ice and mush. I don't like winter much; I turn into too much of a recluse. I become remote. Except for the company of my dogs and weekend visits with my parents and Scarlett I lived a solo life.

I thought again of Siegfried. Why did he have to die? Why couldn't he be here to play with me in the snow and protect me from the suspicions of overgrown detectives? I never would have moved Wilde's body if Siegfried had been alive. I would have run to him for help and we would have faced the music together.

Now that I was good and sorry for myself I didn't hear Scarlett talking to me.

"Violetta, snap out of it! We'll give you and Hugo a ride home, get in, please."

Peter had pulled up and was waiting.

"Thanks, guys, but I need some air, I'm going to walk for a while and then take the bus the rest of the way." I'd walk to Addison, a nice chilly 3 miles and then hop the Addison bus home.

"I can walk with you, Violetta." Hugo looked eager.

"No, absolutely not," I sounded rude and I didn't care. "You go home Hugo and rest. I'm going to walk for a while. I want to be alone."

"Are you sure?" Scarlett asked. She looked uncertain.

"I'm positive," I said. "Go to your antique show, have some fun, forget about this mess for a while."

They left me but not before I saw Hugo's face peering at me from the back window of the Mercedes. I shivered. I started my walk up Lake Shore Drive. Doormen stood in condo driveways looking snappy in their uniforms and there were some really beautiful bronze urns filled with late burgundy and saffron-colored chrysanthemums in front of a stone mansion near Goethe Street. I watched the cars fly by on the Drive and kept sniffing the lake air to clear my head. I wanted to go home and study the photograph in my bag, but I would go to mom and dad's first, collect my dogs and my dirty laundry and then collect my thoughts.

I had only walked up to North Avenue and was cutting across Stockton Drive to take the scenic walk past the Lincoln Park Zoo when the car pulled up besides me. I didn't have to look, *I knew*.

"Violetta," he had rolled down the window and was driving slowly along with me. "Violetta, look at me," he ordered. I gave him a sideways glance and kept walking.

"What do you want?"

"I want to talk to you," he said. I stopped and thought of all I wanted to tell him. Now was as good at time as any.

"And I want to talk to you," I said. I hopped in the car.

"You've got it all wrong," I told him. "Dolly didn't kill Hieronymus."

"No? Then why were the poisons in her purse and why did she conveniently lose the Gucci bag during the memorial service?" He was speaking calmly but I could see his hands tighten on the wheel.

"Dolly may look like a sweet, little old librarian but she's really very smart," I said hotly. "You should read her contribution to the monograph *Cataloging Cultural Objects*," I protested, "it was brilliant."

He permitted his lips to form a small smile. "I'm sure it is riveting bedside reading," he said and gave me a look. I blushed.

"So if she's so brilliant then why did she leave traces of poison in her purse and why did she lose her purse? Isn't that what you're trying to tell me? Why didn't she just throw the bag into an incinerator and be done with it?"

I gasped. "Do you know what that bag is worth? Probably five thousand dollars! What woman would throw away a beautiful Gucci bag given to her by her husband?"

"She probably did try to throw it away and then someone found it and turned it into the concierge," he refuted. "She had already given her keys and phone to her sister, so she could lose the bag."

I thought furiously. "Why did she poison us and herself? She could have been killed. And so could I for that matter!"

"I'm glad you weren't," he said with another look at me. I was getting woozy again. *Couldn't I tame this wanton sex drive of mine when he came around?*

"Dolly probably poisoned herself and the rest of you to divert suspicion away from her. She needed an alibi since everyone seems to have had the time to kill both Wilde and de Winter. So why not get sick from poison? Then we would be sure to look for somebody else. It's a good plan."

"Yes, but she wouldn't have the strength to kill de Winter," I said. "She's not in that good of shape to run a man through with a sword."

"It wouldn't take much strength," he disagreed. "It doesn't take much work to sever a man's jugular vein. It would be just like cutting through a rib eye steak. With a lot more blood."

Yuck. "Yuck," I complained, "must you be so graphic?"

"Sorry," he said. "And we've found out that Dolly Wilde is the sole beneficiary of Wilde's estate, which totals about 4 million dollars."

I whistled. "That much?" I was impressed.

"He had invested some of his patent money quite wisely and some of that art that you were so closely inspecting before stealing things is worth quite a lot of money."

"What did you say?"

"I said some of his art work-"

"Not that bit," I said.

"What did you take, Violetta? I noticed but I didn't want to embarrass you."

"I thought no one saw me," I said, puzzled.

"You yawned and stretched way too loud before you took it," he enlightened me. "The movement called attention to yourself."

"I'll never become a professional pickpocket," I said. "I thought I was hiding my action with a yawn."

"Don't take up a life of crime," he advised me. We drove out of the park, past the Diversey driving range and up Sheridan Road. It was Sunday afternoon and it was peaceful. I leaned back and sighed.

"Feeling better?" he asked me. "Are you going to tell me now?"

"You mean, about what I borrowed?"

"Stole."

"Borrowed."

"So show it," he said.

"Not here, I want you to really listen to me."

"Then I'll take you home and we'll talk."

I felt that ping in my stomach. "OK," I said, "but would you mind stopping at my parents' first? I've got to pick up Samson and Delilah."

Chapter Twenty

Are we not like two volumes of one book?

-Marceline Desbordes-Valmore, 19th century French Poet

When my parents saw Mick they lit up like Christmas trees and tried to ply him with food and drink. He politely declined but said he'd like to take a rain check.

"Anytime," my mother said. "You're always welcome."

"Come into the restaurant tomorrow," Pop said. "I'll make you a Greek omelet, my special." I know that omelet. It's about the size of a football and sautéed in olive oil. It's got *feta, kasseri* and *kefaloteri* cheese, green peppers, olives, artichokes, and if you're lucky he'll throw in some *calamari.* I know an omelet with octopus sounds disgusting but it's really good.

"I'll see if I can make it in," Mick said affably. The men shook hands, my mother gave Mick her special *Italiana* hug and the dogs waited patiently for their leashes. We were once again a cozy little family unit and I was beginning to like it. Maybe after I convinced him Dolly was innocent I could let my hair down again.

We were sitting at my dining room table. I was drinking hot tea and feeding Mick the Grecian chicken that my father had insisted I take home with me. Mick attacked his plate with gusto and I kept the bread basket filled with warm sesame seed bread. He looked tired and worried and there were dark circles under his bright green eyes. I longed to run my fingers through his wavy hair, but we were being official now, weren't we?

Our hands touched as I passed him the plate of olives.

He's not like anybody I know. Big, strong, silent and tough. Could I really get along with a guy like that?

She's cultured, beautiful and crazy as hell. Would I bore her?

He finished a piece of chicken and sighed. "This is delicious. Thank you for feeding me." He leaned back in the chair. "Now, mystery woman, do you want to show me what you think is so important that you had to steal it out of Mrs. Wilde's home?"

I took the photograph out of my hobo bag and handed it to him wordlessly. He looked at it and then at me.

"It's a picture of Hieronymus Wilde. He's very young, thin and has even more tons of hair but it's Wilde, no doubt about it."

I smiled my Cheshire cat smile. "Take another look. Doesn't he remind you of someone?"

Mick held the picture closer to his face. And then he got it.

"Damn, it's Hugo Haydn. What a resemblance. Why didn't we catch it before?"

"We weren't looking for it," I said. "And Wilde's face changed a bit when he got older."

Mick was still holding the photograph up to the light. "This doesn't prove anything, you know. It might be just a coincidence."

"How could it be a coincidence? I know Hugo is Wilde's son, either legitimate or not. Hugo came back," I jumped up and started pacing the dining room, "and tried to establish contact with Daddy. Either Wilde knew about him and got him the job in History or he found out soon after Hugo had started working at the library. Regardless, Wilde didn't want his son under his nose every day so he got him transferred to my department." I took a deep breath.

"So why kill his father?"

"To claim his inheritance. Wilde was worth a lot of money, especially since he sold his patent."

"Why kill de Winter?"

"Mark must have seen Hugo put the arsenic on the cookies or figured it out some way. So Hugo had to kill him. I bet you'll find out that Hugo bought or stole that sword. I just can't believe his nerve in killing Mark in an empty department right before the library opened." Mick was listening to me and I felt a small thrill of gratification.

"And Dolly and the rest of us- he had to get Dolly out of the way so he could step forward as the real heir to the estate. He poisoned himself and me and Roxanne to throw the suspicion elsewhere. He needed to make himself look like a victim and not a suspect."

"It was very risky, if he did that. He could have killed himself. And you, too, Violetta," he said. "I would have gotten him myself if you had been harmed." His eyes turned emerald as they looked at me. I felt his desire. I wanted to throw myself into his arms but I cooled it. *Didn't we have a murderer to catch?*

"Yes, but Hugo is a risk taker. And a liar. He said he went to the University of Illinois library school but I found so many gaps in his knowledge that I wondered what was the matter with him. But now I think if you check with the Graduate School you'll find that he was never enrolled at all."

Mick picked up his phone, made a quick call and gave brief instructions. He got out his BlackBerry and typed away for a minute. I waited patiently, throwing grapes to the dogs.

"So you think he was really trying to kill Dolly," he said.

"He must have given her a bigger dose. And it might have worked but he didn't figure on her having Valium in her system which slowed down the convulsions. The hospital was able to get the activated charcoal down her throat in time. In another hour she might have asphyxiated and died."

He was watching me intently and then he smiled.

"Good work, Holmes."

"Elementary, my dear Watson." I grinned back. "Hug?"

"OK," he said softly. He stood up and enveloped me in his arms. I leaned into his embrace and reeled from the tenderness. *Feel the love.*

"You feel good," he groaned.

"So do you," I said. I wrapped my arms around his broad back and felt the warmth of his muscles. I could smell limes and Grecian chicken. I was becoming intoxicated with the aroma. *Nothing like a 6 foot 8, muscular, wavy-haired cop reeking of limes and garlic to put a girl over the top.* I didn't want to let go.

He let go first. "I've got to stop holding you or I'll never go back to work," he whispered in my ear.

"Don't go back," I said.

"You sure?" he said.

"Absolutely." I was still hanging on to him.

"You were just sick two days ago," he said.

"I'm fine now, and did you know strychnine was an aphrodisiac?"

"The hell it is," he growled. "I'm crazy to be standing here thinking about making love to you when I should be out there working," he said. "You've cast a spell on me like one of your gypsies from the opera."

He wants to make love to me. Yes!

"Would you like to go with me to the opera sometime?"

"I would love to," he said. "I've never been."

"I'll take you to see Trovatore next month," I said. "Lots of gypsies in that one. If we're still speaking," I amended.

"Of course," he agreed smoothly.

He helped me clear the table and stack the dishes in the dishwasher. He put away the butter and cheese without asking. We were getting very domestic and again, I liked it.

"Did Hugo see you take the picture?" he asked me with a serious look.

"I don't think so, but then I didn't think you saw me, either."

He frowned. "You should go back to your parents' house and stay the night," he said. "Until we run a check on Hugo. And until we trace that sword."

"I'm fine here," I said. "I've got to do laundry and I've got to work on the book order before the budget deadline. I'll be OK. Samson and Delilah will protect me." The two pooches were slumped on the dining room floor sleeping. "They're great watchdogs," I added. "They're ferocious like Rottweilers."

He gave me a look that said *I don't think so* but gave in.

"All right, but no walks, just take them out in the yard."

"You think I'm at risk? Then you really think Hugo is responsible for all this?"

"I don't know yet," he admitted. "But it could be a possibility. I'll call you later when I've found out more about him."

I walked him to the front door. He put his hands on my shoulders and gave me a quick massage. I wanted to sink right down on the floor like my dogs. I loved his touch.

"It's such a far-fetched idea," he said to me. "Hugo appearing out of nowhere to get close to his father and then kill him. And then kill his stepmother. If she really was his stepmother? He couldn't be Dolly's son, could he?"

I hadn't thought about that. "I don't know," I said. "But I do know he's a very observant, shrewd young man who puts on a great act of being so cute and innocent." I shivered. "I don't trust him anymore."

"Neither do I," Mick said. "Do not, I repeat, do not open the door to anybody today. Except me and your parents," he amended.

"Do you think Dolly is really responsible for her husband's murder?"

"I think it is the solution that makes the most sense. And the poisons were found in her purse, remember that, Violetta. Eliminate the impossible."

"Anyone could have stolen her purse and planted the poison inside," I argued. "When are you going to bring her in?"

"As soon as the doctors say we can move her." He ran his hands through his hair. "I like Mrs. Wilde and she seems very sweet but then again, I've been fooled many times by people. She might want Wilde's money so she can travel and live a good life without him. She might be fed up with his having a mistress, even though she has been putting on a good act for years. People can snap, Violetta, and do terrible things."

"I know, I've just witnessed some," I said. "I hope you're wrong about Dolly. I hope you drop the charges."

He kissed the top of my head. "Stay well, *koukla*."

I watched him drive away in the unmarked police car. I guess we were making a Greek out of him after all.

Chapter Twenty-One

We can judge the heart of a man by his treatment of animals.

-Immanuel Kant

I was supposed to be working on my book order but I was too jumpy to concentrate. It was getting dark out and I shut all the curtains and turned on all the lights. I changed into my evening uniform, comforting Ramones t-shirt, black leggings, black Birks. I heated up some *avgolemeno* soup and tried to eat. My stomach was still sensitive after my ordeal.

I took the dogs out in the yard for a while and we tossed the tennis ball around. I have a small north side Chicago backyard and there's just enough room for me and the two dogs to run around in circles without tripping into my garden or banging into my Zen fountain that I love to run in the summer.

We went back inside and I jumped when the phone rang.

"Violetta, we're having *bracciole* (Italian meat loaf) for dinner, why don't you come over?" said my mother.

"Thanks, Mom, but I'm not very hungry. I'm going to stay home and work."

"Dad can pick you up later, why don't you spend the night here?"

"I'll call you after dinner," I said. "We can talk about it then." *I know Sophia, she won't take no for answer.*

"Is Mick still there?"

"Yes," I lied. "He's still here."

"Then I'll leave you two in peace," she sounded pleased. She probably had already booked the hall and the *bouzouki* band by now.

I hung up and thought about food. I was hungry. The phone rang again.

"Violetta, am I bothering you?" Scarlett's voice was comforting.

"Of course not, how was the antiques show?"

"Peter bought me a ring," she said in awed tones. "It's so beautiful. It's from the Edwardian era and has opals, diamonds and pearls. I can't believe it."

"Congratulations," I said. "Does this mean you're finally engaged?"

"I think so," she said. "This might be the right time for us."

Think so? She and Beethoven had been together for five years.

"I'm very happy for you, Scarlett. I know how you and Peter feel about each other," I said dutifully. "I hope this is the right time for you two."

"He's such a dear," she cooed. "I'm so happy."

"I'm so glad," I reiterated. *Now if she could just get his mother to like her there might finally be a wedding.* "Scarlett," I said, trying to sound casual, "where did you drop Hugo off?"

"He said he wanted to go home so we dropped him in front of his apartment at Broadway and Belmont," she said.

That was nice of you," I said. *I wondered where he was right now.*

"I wonder how Dolly is," Scarlett said. "She's had a terrible shock today."

"She's probably being sedated after hearing that McGuire wants to arrest her." *He's wrong, I know he's wrong.*

"Maybe she was getting tired of his sleeping with Roxanne," Scarlett mused. "Maybe she snapped."

"I don't believe Dolly did it," I said firmly. "And I can't see her stabbing Mark with a sword."

"Then who did? Maybe Roxanne got tired of Mark pestering her and snapped and killed him."

"I can't see Roxanne shouting "*en garde*!" and stabbing Mark because he was emotionally stalking her. She's the type who would get somebody else to kill him for her," I argued.

"Now that's an idea," Scarlett said. "Dolly killed Hieronymus and Roxanne hired a hit man to kill Mark. It could work that way. Spousal abuse and jealousy are motives."

"Yes, but I just don't think they did it." I wanted to tell her my suspicions about Hugo but now I was wondering if a photograph and an illustrated copy of *The Hounds of the Baskervilles* was enough.

"If it wasn't Dolly then it's someone else, possibly one of us, Violetta. And that's frightening."

"Yes, it is," I agreed. "I can't sleep at night. I wake up in a panic. I keep seeing the faces of Hieronymus and Mark."

"Are you sure you're up to working tomorrow?" she asked me. "Maybe you should take some time off; you have sick days saved up."

"I think I would worry more at home," I said. "I need to keep busy and stay focused. I don't want to brood about this, Scarlett. I went into a deep depression after

Siegfried died and I don't want that to happen again."

"Do you still have your anxiety medication?"

"I keep some around here, but I haven't taken any in months." I looked on top of the refrigerator, in a silver bread basket where I threw all my medicine and vitamins. "Here it is." Buried under the calcium pills and vitamin C was the Paxil and Buspar. *Which one if any?*

"Go take one and lie down for a while," Scarlett said. "I'll call you later."

"Go enjoy yourself," I said. "You've got something to celebrate today."

I put on a CD. Maria Callas in *Rigoletto.* One of my favorite operas. Rigoletto hires Sparafucile to kill the Duke who has soiled the virtue of his daughter, Gilda. At the last minute, Gilda, disguised as a boy, allows herself to be killed instead of the Duke, because of her great gooey love for him. *Women are so damn dumb about men.*

I was humming along with Gilda when Delilah started to bark. That was usually a sign she needed to go so I opened the back door and we went outside again. It was almost dark out and it wasn't even 6pm. It was going to be a long, dull evening. The dogs were sitting quietly in the grass. A cold wind ruffled their curly white hair. I sat on a wrought iron garden bench and brooded for a while. I sneezed and ran inside for a tissue. The phone was blinking and I hit the button to listen to the message.

"Violetta," Mick's voice said. "You were right. The sword has been traced to a store in Schaumburg that sells fencing and martial arts equipment. A man resembling Hugo purchased the sword a month ago. He used the name Jack Stapleton and paid in cash.

Dear God.

"He had dyed his hair brown and altered his appearance with a mustache, but the man recognized him from his pictures that we had digitally manipulated. The D.A. has dropped the charges against Mrs. Wilde. Now we have to find Hugo Haydn. I cannot stress enough, Violetta, be careful! You should stay at your folks tonight. Where are you anyhow?" He sounded annoyed. "Call me the minute you get this message. OK, *koukla.*" He hung up. So did I. I ran back outside to check on my babies.

Samson was standing with his paws on the doggie fence that encircled my yard looking at the big wooden fence that separated my yard from the alley. The back gate was open and Delilah was nowhere to be seen. She must have seen a rabbit and jumped the gate. I hopped over the little wooden picket fence and ran out into the alley. There my heart stopped beating for a second. Hugo Haydn was standing in the alley holding Delilah in his arms!

"Hello, Violetta," he said pleasantly. "You should keep a better eye on your pets; someone might snatch one of the little darlings and feed it to a ravenous pit bull."

Delilah was wriggling and trying to get down. When she saw me she started barking. Samson answered her. If you think that I should have cut and run back into the house and dialed 911 you are wrong. Samson and Delilah are like my kids and I couldn't leave her in the arms of a crazy murderer. I was trying to think of a way to get her out of Hugo's arms and into the yard without us all getting killed but I was stumped. *What did he want of me, anyway?*

"What do you want, Hugo?" I asked.

"I just want to talk to you, Violetta," he said, affably. I found his smiling demeanor more frightening than if he had been frothing at the mouth.

"Put Delilah down and we'll talk," I offered.

"I'll bring her into the house, shall I?" I saw his hands tighten around her neck.

Dear God, don't let him snap her neck. I started to sweat. Delilah gave a frightened whimper. Samson kept barking ferociously.

"Why don't we all take a walk, it's such a nice evening?" I stalled.

"Don't temporize," he said in his prissy reference desk voice. I wanted to smash him right in the face but I didn't want him to hurt my babies. "I don't want to take a walk, I want to come inside and talk to you."

"What about?"

He ignored that. "Why don't you give me some of that nice Greek food like you gave to your policeman boyfriend?"

I made a decision. "OK, I'll feed you. But you've got to put Delilah down."

He walked up to me. I held my breath. I stepped aside and he walked into the garden. I left the gate open and followed him. He stepped over the doggie fence and put Delilah down. She ran by Samson panting heavily. They both ran up the stairs into the house.

Why didn't I have my cell phone in my pocket? What the hell should I do now? Maybe he won't kill you, Violetta; maybe he just wants food and information.

But as I followed him into my house I knew that I would have to fight for my life.

Chapter Twenty-two

Paranoia is knowing all the facts.

-Woody Allen

"You have such a lovely home, Violetta." Hugo was absolutely purring. "Every time I come over I am so impressed." He walked around picking up photographs and the Irving Berlin sheet music on the piano. He peered at my Chevalier posters from the '30s and sighed. "Such good taste you have at home and such bad taste in your wardrobe," he admonished me. "You need a makeover."

"So do you, Hugo," I said. "Those v-neck sweaters and bow ties are sort of '50's aren't they? Why don't we both go on a shopping spree? Why don't we go right now? There's a big sale at Lord and Taylor tonight."

"That's a nice thought, Violetta," he said, walking back into the kitchen. He picked up the lid off the pot of egg lemon soup and lifted the tin foil off the Grecian chicken. "Mmmm- smells good. I'll have some of both, please."

I guess I was stuck feeding him. It would give me more time to figure out what to do next. I got a bowl and plate and started making a tray for him. He was standing by the kitchen island and I said, "Why don't we eat in the dining room? It's more comfortable."

"That's a nice idea, Violetta," he said. He looked pleased like a little kid. I wondered if he had a split personality. *Good librarian, bad librarian?*

"Would you like some wine, Hugo?" I said. *Might as well go the whole route.*

"A small glass would be nice," he said and walked into the dining room. Samson and Delilah sat by my feet. They looked restless. Although I loved them dearly at this moment I wished they were German Shepherds or Dobermans and not 15 pounds each of French charisma. I picked up the Paxil and shook 10 tablets into the soup. I mixed it quickly with a spoon. I hoped the pills would melt quickly or at least be mistaken for grains of rice. I went to serve my guest feeling like Lucrezia Borzia.

I put the wine down in front of Hugo and lit the candles. He was sitting in the same chair that Mick had recently sat in. I couldn't help comparing the two men. One was tall, strong, and a professional catcher of killers, the other was a short, psycho wimp who killed most professionally. *Who could ask for anything more?*

Hugo took a tiny sip of wine. He coughed delicately. He was such a paradox. The dainty eater was a ruthless killer. I realized that we were about the same height and weight and I also realized that I wasn't as afraid as I thought I'd be. If he tried to choke me I could knock him to the floor. Rape was out of the question, I'd annihilate him. But if he pulled a gun or a knife, now that could be tricky. Now that he was here in my dining room eating Pop's soup and Grecian chicken, he didn't seem quite so dangerous.

Talk, get him to talk. Then the meds can kick in and maybe he'll pass out on you.

I poured more wine in his glass and poured a glass for me.

"How did you know that I was Hieronymus' son?" he asked me. I held my breath as he stirred his soup and then took a healthy spoonful.

"I didn't know for a long time," I said. "I thought maybe you were a son of one of Wilde's former flames. I wondered why you showed up so suddenly in our department. Frankly, Hugo- you weren't very good at being a librarian. Our college students know more about reference books than you do."

"I was a biology major before I quit college," he said. "I'm not much into books."

"How about poisons?"

"Biology was very useful to me," he admitted.

"So I didn't suspect you of anything. Until I saw the picture of Hieronymus as a very young man. Then I realized how much you two resembled each other. How did you know I knew?"

He took another sip of wine. "I saw you take the picture at Dolly's. I knew something was up then."

I nodded and took the plunge. "Did you really kill your father?"

"Indeed I did."

"How did you get the arsenic?"

"I used to work on a cruise ship. We made many stops in the Caribbean and South America. Drugs are easy to get there," he shrugged and dipped some bread in the soup. Part of a pill clung to the bread. I watched him devour it.

"Did you ever take any library classes?"

"Of course not, do you think I would take up such a wimpy profession? You librarians are really weird."

Look who's talking.

"How did you get the job? From your father?"

"Daddy dearest felt it was in his best interest to get his only son a decent job in the library. I gave him some bogus transcripts and he was able to convince Mrs.

Vandermeer that I was the next bright young thing to illuminate the information science field. I was waiting for him to announce our relationship and welcome me into the bosom of his family. But it never happened."

"He didn't want to acknowledge you?"

"No, he didn't want to admit to having a by-blow, a child born on the wrong side of the blanket, as it were. He didn't want to sully his patrician name and upset the dear, wronged Dolly. He just wanted to carry on as before, collecting art, being a guru and banging as many chicks as possible."

I cringed at the last sentence.

"Sorry, Violetta, my language is getting a little crude."

"I prefer not to think about Wilde's sex life."

"Dad was amazing and had all the notches in his belt to prove it. He was very proud of his sexual acumen. I guess we should get the makers of Viagra to erect a stone monument in the middle of Grant Park in his honor. Don't you think?" He ate quickly like a bird, eating bits of chicken and wiping his mouth after each bite. Samson and Delilah had perked up when they smelled the food. They watched Hugo eating.

"Can't you teach your dogs it's not polite to beg?"

"Samson, Delilah, get back," I ordered. "I'll get them a treat." I stood up and headed for the kitchen, wine glass glued to my tense hand.

"Don't trust me, Violetta?" Hugo called out pleasantly. "Do you think I'll drop a little strychnine into your Roditis wine?"

I came back with a bag of dog treats. I put my glass down with a thump.

"Something like that." My eyes widened. On the table near Hugo's left hand, was a small hand gun. It was very black and shiny like a toy. I ignored it.

"It's a 38 Special," he said. "Isn't it cute?" I ignored that, too.

"Did you kill Mark de Winter?"

"Of course. He had figured out my paternity a month ago and he had heard Wilde and me arguing in the stacks. After Wilde died he called me at home that night. He said he had seen me tampering with the cookies and knew that I had killed him. At first I didn't believe him, I thought I was too quick for anyone to spot me, but I knew that he had enough on me to get me arrested. So I told him to meet me in the library next morning and I would give him some emeralds I had picked up in Colombia. This was to be my first installment to assure his silence. After I inherited Wilde's wealth I told him that there would be enough for him to retire and take that precious ice queen Roxanne with him around the world."

"And he believed you?" I was incredulous. Mark couldn't have been that dumb.

"Librarians read too many novels," Hugo smirked. He finished the soup and I exhaled, the first time in seconds. "They have a childish belief that life imitates fiction." He put his hand over the gun and leaned in my direction. "Well, they're wrong. Fiction imitates *life.*"

"So you met Mark in my department at the crack of dawn and then what? Walked up to him calmly and ran him through with a sword? Wasn't that a bit melodramatic?"

He smiled and finished his wine. I picked up the bottle and filled up our glasses. Let him talk and get drunk and I hoped to hell the pills would knock him out soon.

"I thought it was a nice touch. He had been nicked by dear old Dad in a fencing duel and now he met his end by the same sword. Or as like a replica as I could get. I had bought it a while ago because I was planning to run the old man through and frame Mark. But I changed my mind. I liked the arsenic better. It's a more painful way to die. And I detest blackmailers. No integrity there, my dear. Poor old Mark. I especially liked the fact that he was killed right under the name *Dumas* that glittered overhead. Wouldn't the Musketeers be proud of me?" His face was getting a bit flushed and he said Mush-ke-teers. *I hoped he was getting looped.*

"You're a very clever man, Hugo," I said. *Keep him talking.*

"I'm smarter than all of you librarians put together," he said. "And more talented. Did you know I worked as a magician during the summers with my dear old alcoholic auntie who raised me? She was the black sheep of the family; Hieronymus wouldn't even mention her name. I learned a lot watching her and her cohorts. I have very quick hands. Quick for running de Winter through with an epée, quick for sprinkling arsenic on Wilde's food and quick for spiking the shrimp at the hotel Friday night."

"I never saw you do anything," I admitted.

"The hand is quicker than the eye, dear Violetta," he said, and picked up the gun.

Chapter Twenty-Three

A creature of infinite patience and craft, with a smiling face and a murderous heart.

-The Hound of the Baskervilles, Sir Arthur Conan Doyle

"What possible reason would you have to kill me, Hugo? We have always been friends."

"Friends?" he sneered at me. "You were just tolerating me, Violetta. I might have been something more to you, but you have been living in a psychedelic haze thinking about that dead husband of yours. Why don't you get a t-shirt made with his face plastered all over your chest?" He laughed; a high girlish cackle.

"I'm not going to sit here and listen to you insult Siegfried," I said coolly, rising from my seat.

He picked up the gun. "Sit down. I said, sit down! I'm not going to shoot you first, Violetta, I'm going to shoot Samson and then Delilah," he waved the gun at my dogs and giggled, "Or is it the other way around, Delilah and Samson?" I sat down. I felt sick now. Here I was sitting with a pathological killer who would enjoy shooting my dogs in front of me and watching me writhe in agony as they died. I felt emotions surging over me-shock, fear and then a blazing anger. If he killed my dogs, then he and I would both die, pretty damn quick.

"Hugo, if you hurt my dogs, we're both going to die. I will kill you barehanded."

I must have sounded beyond serious because he sat up and looked upset.

"Violetta, temper, temper, geez you Italians and Greeks are all emotion! I'm not going to hurt your dogs, darling, not if you do what I want."

"And what do you want, dear Hugo?"

"I want to get out of town. I want you to drive me to the bus station because I'm leaving tonight."

"Where do you want to go?" I said.

"Anywhere, far away from here. You don't need an I.D. at the Greyhound Bus Station."

"Don't you think the police are watching the airport, the trains and the buses leaving town?"

"For me?" he seemed incredulous. "For little ole' cotton pickin' me? Why Violetta, honey, I am the master of disguise. I'll darken my hair and paste on a little goatee mustache, put on my jeans and boots and a bandanna and when I sling my guitar over my shoulder you'll think I'm just a little country boy going home to visit my granny in old Memphis, Tennessee," he drawled. "Just like Elvis."

The man was insane. Did he know that they had recognized him at the weapons store?

He waved the gun in my face again. "After I'm done eating, you're going to drive me home. With your doggies. Then I can change my clothes, grab my stuff and hit the road."

"They traced the sword to you, Hugo," I said. "The man recognized you from pictures the police showed him at the weapons store. I think you should give yourself up."

He laughed uproariously, slamming his fist on the table. Wine spilled out of his glass and slopped on the table. The dogs sat up and cocked their ears at his high pitched laughter. I hoped he was feeling the effects of the Paxil. *Maybe I should try and get him out of here? Play along with his far-fetched scheme to take the bus out of town?*

"I will never give myself up," he said. "I will die first." He scratched his nose with the butt of the gun. I wished it would go off in his smug face. And why the hell didn't McGuire call me back?

"That was very clever of you using the name Jack Stapleton," I said, stalling for time.

"Right out of *The Hound of the Baskervilles,*" Hugo said with a big yawn. "I picked the name of the man and secret heir who wanted to kill Sir Henry. And did you like the way I call myself Hugo?"

I thought about it and nodded.

"Sir Hugo Baskerville, debauchery and excess killed him, didn't it?"

"Yes, but it won't kill me," he said rubbing his side with the gun. "My stomach feels queasy, I ate too much of this greasy Greek food," he complained.

Pop's food is not greasy.

"What is your real name?" I asked. "Do you want some ginger ale?" Maybe I could pour a few more tranqs down his throat.

"My real name is Leonard, but I changed it to Leonardo, it's classier," Hugo said. "But I'm still Hugo for a while." He rubbed his cheek on his shoulder. "Better give me that ginger ale," he said. "I don't feel so good."

I walked into the kitchen, grabbed a pop out of the refrigerator and took a glass from the shelf. By the time I got back to the dining room, Hugo had his head down on the table and appeared to be fast asleep. Samson and Delilah had gone into the living room as far away from Hugo as they could go. I stood and listened. I could hear him breathing. Was he asleep? Could I take the gun from his hand? Had the pills kicked in?

I tiptoed closer, one, two, three baby steps. I leaned over and gently put one finger on the gun, then another. I started to pull the gun out of his grasp but he jumped up and screamed- “surprise! Fooled you, Violetta,” and then hit me on the side of the head with the gun. I saw lights and heard a roaring in my ears and then I fell down on the dining room carpet.

When I came to moments later, Samson and Delilah were licking my face and Hugo was trying to put an ice cube on my head. He reeked of wine and Grecian chicken. I sat up quickly, knocking the ice out of his hand.

“What did you do that for?”

“You were trying to take my gun, naughty, naughty Violetta,” he giggled.

“Are you smoking crack?”

“Temper, temper,” he admonished, waving the gun under my nose. “Come on now, you’ve got to be a good girl and drive me to the bus station. Behave yourself and I won’t hit you again,” he said.

My head hurt like hell. I felt a trickle of sweat running down my cheek but when I touched it my fingers were red. I was bleeding; the bastard had cut my face.

“Get me a tissue or a towel, I’m bleeding,” I said. I groaned and sat up.

Hugo went into the bathroom and came out with a box of tissue. I mopped up the best I could. I had a headache and was tiring of this situation.

“All right, let’s get out of here,” I said. “I suppose I can’t call my mother and father and tell them I’m going to visit Scarlett?”

"And have you talk in Greek or Italian and alert them what's going on? I don't think so." His sleepiness had worn off and now he was wired for sound. "Get your coat."

I got my cape. "Can you please let the dogs stay here? They don't understand what's going on. Let them stay home. Come on, Hugo, they can't talk."

He looked down at my babies. "No, bring them. You'll behave better with them along."

I put the dogs on their leashes and waited.

"OK, let's move it. I'm going to be walking right behind you, Violetta." He moved closer and stuck the gun right in the small of my back. "I'll be near you every step of the way. Don't try anything weird or I'm going to shoot you, I swear to God."

"Are you that desperate?"

"*Tempt not a desperate man*," he quoted.

"Leave Shakespeare out of this," I said. "You're not much of a Romeo."

"Don't be bitchy, Violetta, or you'll never hook up with that enormous Irishman." He seemed to think this was funny and went into a paroxysm of laughter mixed with dry, hacking coughs. I managed to lock the front door while hanging onto two dogs and feeling the pressure of the gun at my back.

"Do you have to crowd me, Hugo? I can't move with you pushing into me."

"Too bad," he snarled. "Open the car."

I unlocked the car and put the dogs in the back seat. Hugo stuck to me like honey on a *baklava.*

"Give me the car keys and get in the car," he said. "If you try to run away I'm going to kill your dogs before I drive away forever." He grabbed the keys from my hand. "Hurry up and get in," he ordered. "I'm watching your every move."

I got in but not before I saw two men hiding behind a parked car across the street. I hoped they were cops but with my luck they would probably turn out to be muggers.

"Where to, boss?" I said lightly. Hugo was starting to look like hell.

"Start the car, let's go. Forget taking me home, just head out to the bus station. Do you know where it is?"

"Somewhere west of Greek town," I ventured. "Harrison Street and Desplaines?"

"Just get there," he said and settled back in the seat. He looked exhausted. His breath was heavy and a foul odor filled the car. I sniffed. *Was it the dogs or Hugo?*

I was driving east down Addison. I figured if I took Clark Street I might be able to rear end a cop car or drive into a picnic table outside of the Wiener's Circle. Maybe I could attract enough attention to get pulled over and get me and the dogs safely out of the car. How I could accomplish this with a maniac holding a gun to my side was not entirely clear at the moment but I was praying that fate would offer me an opportunity.

We passed Southport Avenue and drove past two-flats, condos and homes with the ubiquitous Cubs stickers in the windows. There was a dark car with two men in it behind us and I prayed they were cops. As we approached the Cubby Bear Lounge Hugo gripped my arm.

"I don't feel so good," he moaned. "Park the car. I think I'm going to be sick. I need a bathroom. What the hell was in that chicken anyway?"

"It must have been the garlic," I said. If I told him I had OD'ed him on Paxil he would probably whack me again. Usually you can't park around here but it being a Sunday night we were able to find a spot. I parallel parked the Beetle in one quick stroke. "Now what?"

"Get out," he ordered. "Give me the keys. Leave the dogs in here."

The car with the two guys passed us and pulled into the McDonald's parking lot across the street from the Cubby Bear. I got out of the car and waited. Hugo motioned with the gun for me to walk around to his side. My dogs watched me anxiously from the window. Hugo got out and immediately pushed the gun into my ribs.

"Walk," he said. He looked terrible. His skin was pale and clammy and he kept blinking like he had sand in his face. I was sure the pills were working by now. I wondered how long it would take to knock him out completely. We walked up the street past the Taco Bell and at the door of the Cubby Bear he pulled me inside.

"Ten bucks," the guy at the door said.

"What's the show?" I asked him. *Like I cared at this point.*

The guy pointed his thumb at a poster behind his head.

"Retro punk night," he told us. "Phil n' the Blanks, Bohemia and the Lawn Chairs. Punk bands from the '80's. You want in? You're holding up the line."

Hugo pulled a twenty out of his pocket. He was still glued to my side. His other hand had found its way through the slit in my cape and I could feel the gun pressing against my right breast. He was leaning quite heavily on me and the bouncer looked at us funny.

"Is your friend drunk?"

I nodded no. The guy stamped our hands and let us in.

Inside the place was very crowded. It was indeed punk night and a large assortment of old and young punks had come to pay homage to the bands of the past. Up on stage were the Lawn Chairs and I had to admit for a bunch of 50-something rockers, they had held up pretty well. The lead singer was part Blondie-part Elvira with spiky black hair and cheekbones that rivaled David Bowie. The dance floor was crowded and Hugo pulled me into the middle of the mosh pit and told me to dance.

"I can't dance in here," I complained. "I can't even breathe."

But Hugo had grabbed my other arm and was doing some kind of funky punk Polka with me. The gun kept banging into my side.

"*My bosses give me lots of coffee-*
Says it make my fingers faster.
If I don't keep myself in orbit-
My life will be a real disaster!" Sang the David Bowie chick on stage.

My life was a disaster, I could relate to that.

"Let's go over there," Hugo said, "I feel sick, I'm going to vomit all over my shoes and I want to use the john."

"Go ahead, I won't stop you," I said, but he had his arms around me now and we were walking to the back of the club. Somewhere between the guys with Mohawks and the girls with pink hair I saw a couple of faces that I recognized. Halliday was standing behind the bar and I saw Mick at the entrance with a couple of plain-clothes cops. They were keeping their distance.

"You're taking me in with you," he shouted over the music.

"They won't let you in the ladies room," I shouted back. "Too many people around."

"Then we'll go in the men's room!" He pulled me into the bathroom with him and quickly shoved us both into a stall. There were two guys in the bathroom and they both laughed and left. No help there.

I was getting tired of this shit. If Hugo was going to puke, I was going to stuff his head down the toilet. But he kept standing there smiling at me. We were inches away from each other in a urine scented graffiti decorated stall with pools of water under our feet.

"So, what now?" I said.

"I'm going to take a whiz."

"In front of me?" I was indignant.

"Why not? You've seen it before," he said and calmly unzipped his pants with one hand while pointing the gun straight at my heart with the other.

I squeezed my eyes half shut. I didn't want to look. I had been traumatized enough tonight without having to stare at Hugo-Leonard's jewels. Where was Mick? *Why didn't he storm right in here and save me?*

Hugo finally stopped peeing and arranged his pants with one hand. The bathroom door opened and a man walked in. He entered the next stall. Hugo put his fingers up to his lips. We waited for a long time and then the man flushed the toilet and left. Hugo passed his hand across his forehead.

"I'm sweating like a pig," he complained. "I think I've got the flu."

I didn't reply. He would need to take some activated charcoal very soon. His eyes were getting glassy and he was speaking as if he were drunk. His hold on the gun, however, never faltered.

The bathroom door opened again and this time a couple more guys walked in. I heard a stall door swing open and shut and saw feet standing at the urinals. I wanted to shout for help, but I was terrified of Hugo and his snub nose revolver. I wanted to see my parents again and my dogs. I wanted to pick up with Mick where we had left off.

Next thing I heard was a voice. "So how ya doing?" said a man in great South Side tones. I looked up and saw a guy smiling down at us. Hugo looked up in shock and the man jumped over the top of the stall. As this was happening the stall door was ripped off its hinges, people were shouting and Hugo's gun went off.

I never knew how many people could fit in a bathroom stall but tonight I found out. There seemed to be a hundred guys stuffed in this 3 by 3 area with me stuck in the middle. After Mr. Travis Bickle (as I liked to think of him) jumped over the stall knocking Hugo to the ground the entire Chicago Police Department came in *en masse*.

The gun flew into the toilet and the bullet struck the overhead light fixture shattering it into a thousand pieces. We were covered with toilet water, (Hugo hadn't flushed, yuck!) broken glass and sweat. I felt little cool glass shards covering my face and flying down my Elvis tee and I think I swallowed one. Hugo was dragged out screaming by two cops and I was left alone feeling like I was going to be blinded like Oedipus. Just when I was going to start screaming myself, Mick McGuire walked into the stall.

"Violetta, *koukla,* come to me, are you all right?" He was gently brushing my clothes with a handkerchief (where did he get that?) and holding me in the crook of his arm, like I was truly loved. I melted in his embrace and when he took a feather duster (and where did he get that?) and brushed my face, getting off any bits of remaining glass before he gave me a quick, gentle kiss, did I then finally break down and burst into tears.

Chapter Twenty-Four

"Oh, me name is Mick McGuire and I'll quickly tell to you, of a young girl I admired named Katie Donahue, she was fair and fat and 40 and believe me when I say, that whenever I came in at the door, you could hear her Mammy say-"

-Irish Folksong

It was after midnight and we were sitting in my mother's kitchen eating and drinking. Again. I was eating hot, flaky *tiropitas* (little cheese pies) and swilling ouzo. The strong anise flavored liqueur burned the back of my throat as I swallowed. I coughed and Mick gently patted my back.

"Easy now, darling," he said. "Take smaller sips, don't throw it back now." He was eating apple pie and drinking a huge glass of milk. I like the concept of milk but as I told you before, I'm lactose intolerant. "Why don't you have a sip of milk? It will cut the alcohol." He held his glass to my lips.

"I'm lactose intolerant," I said, taking another swig of *ouzo*.

"Really? No milk, ice cream, cheese? Hey, I've seen you eat Greek cheese, Violetta. Greek cows don't count?" He was smiling and hanging on my shoulder and I stared at him in shock. I had never seen him so cute and boyish and so silly.

"Are you sure you haven't hit the Paxil?" I asked him. "You seem so happy."

"I am happy. We caught Hugo, Mrs. Wilde can be left in peace if her sisters don't sue the city for false arrest, you and your dogs are safe- Violetta, all's right with the world." He did look very content. "I'm glad you remembered to tell us that you had dropped the pills in old Hugo Baskerville's soup," he added. "Otherwise we would have had one very stiff murderer on our hands."

"Did I tell you about Hugo Baskerville?" After all this confusion, I couldn't remember.

He held up his BlackBerry. "I downloaded *The Hound of the Baskervilles* today and read it. Cool story. You were right about the family resemblance and greed. You were right about de Winter blackmailing Hugo. In fact, you were right about everything." He leaned in closer and started taking the pins out of my hair. My mother sat stirring her coffee, smiling. My father was cooking a calamari omelet- the smell of octopus stunk up the house. My dogs sat waiting for something to drop. They love calamari. French dogs eating Greek food, go figure.

"It's done!" my father flourished an enormous omelet pan filled with his specialty. "Who wants to eat?"

That was a statement, not a question and my dad filled two plates with healthy amounts of octopus omelet. Could Mick eat octopus after apple pie? He could and did. He swallowed a forkful of the concoction and smiled.

"It's delicious, Mr. Aristotle, you are a master chef."

My dad looked pleased. "*Efharisto*- thank you, eat it in good health." He stood there beaming at us. He would have stood there and made sure we gobbled up every bite but my mother had other ideas.

"Sam, I think we should go to bed," she said.

"Now? But they're going to eat!"

My mother looked at my father, looked at Mick and me sitting close together eating octopus omelet, shot another look at my father, and without pointing made him see my loose hair and probably soon to be loose morals. My father got it.

"You're right, Sophia, I am tired," he yawned magnificently. "There's been too much excitement today. Let's go to bed. You're sleeping here Violetta, right?"

No, no, no, I want to go home and have Mick tuck me in.

"I think I want to go home, Pop. I am going to work tomorrow," I said firmly.

Three voices raised in protest.

"No, you should stay home and rest!" said my father.

"Violetta darling, take a couple of days off," my mother urged.

"Are you sure you want to go in there tomorrow?" Mick asked. "You've been through hell this week, *koukla*." He touched the bandage on my temple where the gun had hit me.

After hearing that Greek term of endearment my mother took my dad by the arm and pulled him out of the kitchen. "Good night, Violetta, Good night Mick," she said. "We'll leave you to figure things out."

My father followed her petite figure out meekly. "Eat before it gets cold," he said and left us.

I put down my fork.

"Not hungry?"

"Not anymore," I said.

He dropped his fork on the plate. "Me neither, but I didn't want to hurt your father's feelings by not finishing this."

I got up and found a restaurant style silver carton for bringing food home. I gently pushed the remains of his plate and the remaining omelet in the pan into the carton.

"You can bring this home and eat it for breakfast tomorrow," I said. "Would you mind taking me home?"

"Are you sure you don't want to stay here with your folks?" he asked me. He came close to me and finished taking out the rest of the hairpins. My wild locks tumbled past my shoulders.

"No, I want to go home," I told him. I leaned against him and shut my eyes.

"You shouldn't be alone tonight," he said softly. His voice was a caress, his body was beyond comfort.

"I won't be alone, will I?" I looked up into his eyes.

"No, *koukla*, you won't."

"Opaaaaaaaaa," I said and threw my dogs a piece of calamari. They loved octopus.

The End

to be continued............

RECIPES

Kourabiedes

Greek butter cookies with cloves

Prep Time: 30 minutes

Cook Time: 30 minutes

Ingredients:

- 4 cups of butter
- 2 cups of confectioner's sugar
- 2 egg yolks
- 2 teaspoons of vanilla extract
- 2 teaspoons of baking powder
- 3 tablespoons of brandy or Greek Metaxa
- 1 cup of coarsely chopped roasted almonds
- 12 cups of all-purpose flour
- 1-2 pounds of confectioner's sugar (for dusting)
- cloves

Preparation:

Start with all ingredients at room temperature.

In a mixing bowl, cream the butter and sugar until white. Dissolve the baking powder in the brandy and slowly add to mixture, along with egg yolks, vanilla, and almonds. Add flour gradually. Knead the dough by hand until malleable.

Preheat oven to 350F (175C).

Shape the cookies by hand into dome-shaped circles about 2 inches in diameter and 3/4 inch thick, insert clove, and place on a lightly buttered cookie sheet. Bake for 20 minutes at 350F (175C) until cookies barely start to brown.

While cookies are baking, sift confectioner's sugar onto a large tray or cookie sheet. As soon as the cookies are done, sprinkle with rose water (optional), roll in the sugar. When all the cookies have been coated once, repeat (without rose water) and cool. When cooled, place in layers on a serving platter that has been dusted with sugar, sift a liberal amount of sugar on each layer.

Yield: 60 cookies

Avgolemono Soup (Egg-lemon)

4 cups basic chicken stock [for a vegetarian soup, use Garlic Broth]
6 tablespoons (90 g) Carolina or other long-grain white rice
8 egg yolks
1/4 cup (65 ml) fresh lemon juice
coarse salt, to taste
freshly ground black pepper, to taste

Preparation

In a medium saucepan, bring the stock to a boil. Stir in the rice and cook until tender, about 8 to 10 minutes.

Meanwhile, beat the egg yolks and lemon juice together in a large bowl using a whisk. Practice saying opaa while mixing.

When the rice is tender, slowly ladle half of the hot broth into the yolks to temper them, whisking constantly. Whisk the egg yolk mixture into the broth and place over low heat. Cook, stirring constantly, just long enough to thicken the soup. Do not boil. Season to taste with salt and pepper.

Honey Butter

Take a carton of whipped butter, put in a bowl, keep adding honey until it's all soft and gooey and mixed up and then add a generous dollop of Jack Daniel's, Metaxa or Jameson's and some ground vanilla bean. Eat with everything.

Also from MX Publishing

Close To Holmes

A Look at the Connections Between Historical London, Sherlock Holmes and Sir Arthur Conan Doyle.

Eliminate The Impossible

An Examination of the World of Sherlock Holmes on Page and Screen.

The Norwood Author

Arthur Conan Doyle and the Norwood Years (1891 - 1894)

Also From MX Publishing

In Search of Dr Watson

Wonderful biography of Dr.Watson from expert Molly Carr.

Arthur Conan Doyle, Sherlock Holmes and Devon

A Complete Tour Guide and Companion.

The Lost Stories of Sherlock Holmes

Eight more stories from the pen of John H Watson – compiled by Tony Reynolds.

www.mxpublishing.com

Also From MX Publishing

Aside Arthur Conan Doyle

A collection of twenty stories from ACD's close friend Bertram Fletcher Robinson.

Bertram Fletcher Robinson

The comprehensive biography of the assistant plot producer of The Hound of The Baskervilles

Wheels of Anarchy

Reprint and introduction to Max Pemberton's thriller from 100 years ago. One of the first spy thrillers of its kind.

Also From MX Publishing

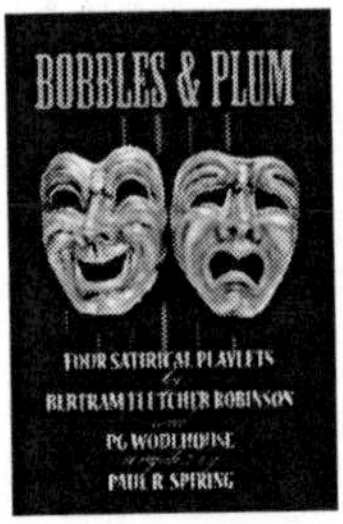

Bobbles and Plum

Four playlets from PG Wodehouse 'lost' for over 100 years – found and reprinted with an excellent commentary

The World of Vanity Fair

A specialist full-colour reproduction of key articles from Bertram Fletcher Robinson containing of colour caricatures from the early 1900s.

Tras Las He huellas de Arthur Conan Doyle (in Spanish)

Un viaje ilustrado por Devon.

CPSIA information can be obtained at www.ICGtesting.com
226838LV00003B/106/P

9 781908 218407